A HOPELESS HEIST

A HOPE WALKER MYSTERY BOOK 2

DANIEL CARSON

Published by Daniel Carson Books

Cover Design by Alchemy Book Covers

Editing by David Gatewood

Editing by Tristi Pinkston

CHAPTER 1

I found the note near the front door of the Library, the bar where I lived. Someone must have slipped it under the door. It was a half sheet of paper torn from some journal or notebook. The letters were formed in blue ink, and the words had a simple message.

I didn't mean to do it.

I unlocked the deadbolt on the front door, stepped out onto Main Street, and looked both ways. Nobody was running. Nobody looked suspicious at all.

It was early Saturday morning, and Hopeless, Idaho, was taking its time waking up.

I stepped back into the Library and looked at the note again.

Never meant to do what? And why was the note slipped under the Library's front door?

It seemed somebody wanted me to solve a mystery.

Too bad.

I needed to kidnap someone first.

Now, to be clear, I'd never kidnapped someone before.

I once stole a hamster from the back of Mrs. Nettle's third-grade classroom and set him free behind our school. I even stuffed Gemima Clark in a locker after she told the entire cafeteria that I was named Hope because my family sure "Hoped" I'd grow boobs one day. (For the record, I did. Not very big boobs. But they were there. Promise.)

But I'd never, ever kidnapped anyone.

The way it happened in the movies was always the same. Van pulls up. Door slides open. Masked guys jump out.

They make it look so easy.

But as I pulled up in front of my best friend Katie's house, I knew nothing about this was going to be easy. I'd arranged everything with her husband, Chris, and it was meant to be a bit of a surprise. I was taking Katie for an early Saturday morning hike. Of course, Katie would never go hiking with me in a million years. She'd rather get acupuncture from a blind elephant. I know because that's exactly what she said a week ago when I suggested we go hiking sometime.

So, Chris and I had a cover story. I was picking her up to hit some garage sales, and Chris would stay home to watch the kids. I'd even grabbed her a coffee from A Hopeless Cup to sweeten the deal. But Katie Rodgers was no dummy, and I could tell she was suspicious when she opened the door that morning.

"Hello, Hope," was all she said before she scanned my outfit. I saw the terror in her eyes as soon as she saw my stretchy pants and my jogging shoes. She spun around and ran up the stairs, screaming, "No!"

She barricaded herself in her bedroom and yelled that she had *known* this was a dirty trick. The Hope Walker she knew would *never* agree to early morning garage sale-ing. And furthermore, hell would have to freeze over before she would come out of that room and go—gasp!—*exercising* with me.

I was trying to kidnap her. That's what she screamed through the door. Kidnap her.

Kidnap was a strong word. More like . . . encouragement with extreme prejudice.

That brings us to the locked bedroom door. I leaned toward Chris. "How long can she hold out?"

"She's got a box of Ritz crackers under the bed and a pack of juice boxes somewhere in the closet."

"Plus access to a bathroom and cable TV."

Chris nodded grimly. "I'd say you have your work cut out for you."

Their baby, Celia, started crying downstairs. Chris sighed. "Duty calls. Let me know if I need to call the fire department so they can bring the Jaws of Life."

I turned to Dominic, Katie's five-year-old son and occasional menace to society. "Does your mom ever lock herself in her room when your dad's gone?" I asked.

"Only when Grandma's coming over or Lucy makes the world's most annoying sound."

"What's the world's most annoying sound?"

Dominic smiled. "Show 'em, Luce."

Six-year-old Lucy puffed out her chest and stuck her neck out like a rooster. A high-pitched alien sound rocketed out of her throat.

I covered my ears and yelled for her to stop.

"Okay, Dominic," I said when the unbearable sound had ceased. "How do you normally get your mom out of her room?"

He shrugged. "I have some great ideas. But everything I want to do, Lucy always says no."

"Like what?"

"I wanted to throw Dad's bowling ball through the door."

"Okay. Creative. I guess Lucy didn't want you to ruin the door?"

"No, she said we wouldn't be able to lift the ball."

"Smart girl."

"Then there were the smoke bombs."

"Let me guess. Lucy said you didn't have any matches."

Dominic and Lucy laughed. "No, silly. She said we might burn the house down."

No wonder Katie locked herself in her room from time to time.

"Do you still have any of those smoke bombs left?" I asked.

Dominic's eyes got big. "You mean we can use them?"

"Possibly. Unless you think I can break the door down."

"Mama sometimes moves the dresser in front of the door," Lucy said.

"In that case, I'm definitely gonna need those smoke bombs."

An anguished sound came from the bedroom, followed by a clicking at the doorknob and the door flying open. Katie narrowed her eyes at Dominic.

"You light a smoke bomb in this house and you won't get pancakes until you're twenty."

Dominic made a face, and he and Lucy ran down the stairs.

Katie turned her wrath on me. "So, you and Chris. My best friend and my own husband. Conspiring against me."

"You did say you wanted to start exercising again."

Katie threw her hands up in the air. "I didn't *mean* it, Hope! It's just the kind of thing you say. Like, oh, I should eat less sugar, or I should go to the funeral, or I should really take care of this yeast infection one of these days."

"You really should do all of those things."

"Who asked you?"

"Listen, I know it's been hard to take off the baby weight."

"You calling me fat?"

"You think your best friend would call you fat?"

"I don't know, because it sort of feels like that's what you're doing."

"You said you wanted to exercise. And for the record, I don't think you're fat. But . . ."

Katie rolled her eyes. "Here it comes."

"Just listen. I think you're *stressed*. Unbelievably stressed."

"How can you tell?"

"You just ate an entire sleeve of Ritz crackers."

"Anybody could do that," she said, crumbs falling from her lips. "They're super yummy."

"I'm pretty sure you ate the plastic too."

"Oh," she said, pulling a bit of plastic from the corner of her mouth. "I maybe see your point."

I patted her on the shoulder. "Chris is worried about you."

She threw her hands up in the air again. "So now *Chris* is calling me fat?"

"Nobody's calling you fat. But you have a bunch of little kids, one of them has a fairly impressive arsenal of munitions, one is a baby who craps all day, and the other makes a noise from her throat that will give me nightmares for the next month."

"Yeah. It *is* pretty horrifying."

"And exercise can help with that."

"It can? Because it sounds like exercise is just the poop topping on the rest of that crap sundae you just described."

"No, Katie. Exercise is magical. It creates these tiny little candy-like sprinkles called endorphins. Endorphins will make you feel better. Not as stressed."

"Endorphins sound like the kind of thing skinny people make up to get fat people more interested in exercising."

"It won't even feel like exercising. Just a little hike."

"You really are kidnapping me, aren't you?"

"Just a short stretch of the legs. But first, we need to visit Stank."

* * *

THE BELL CLANGED against the glass as Katie and I pushed open the front door to Stank's Hardware and I took in one of my favorite spots from my youth. Granny and Bess were always dragging me to Stank's to get something for either the Library or the house. The wide wooden planks on the floor looked like they were a hundred years old, and they sloped from the front of the store to the back. I once let a marble loose near the front door, and it made it all the way into the restroom. It had to be some kind of world record.

Stank still had tufts of hair that rimmed his ears, although it was grayed now, no longer the dark hair I remembered from my youth. A large pair of glasses sat perched upon his nose as he eyed the back of a package of nails.

When he saw Katie and me, he jumped to his feet. "I don't believe it," he said. He hustled around the counter, hobbled my way, and gave me a big hug.

"Nice to see you too, Stank."

"We've missed you in these parts, Hope Walker."

"The only reason I'm back is because of you. Please tell me you're still single."

Stank blushed, and for a moment I thought the big guy might have a coronary. "Now you're just teasing me."

"I see Cup's still in business. The question is, are you and Cup still in business?"

Stank, of Stank's Hardware, had once upon a time had a torrid affair with Cup, the owner of Cup's Cakes. I was wondering if the two of them were still an item.

Stank blushed again, but then he cracked a smile. "A gentleman does not kiss and tell."

Katie laughed. "Stank Neederman, you sly old dog."

"Emphasis on the 'old' part." Then his eyes lit up and he held up a hand. "Hold on just a second, Hope. I've got something in back for you."

He turned around and hustled down the hallway at the back of his store.

"I still can't believe you got me up this early to hike," Katie said.

"You're a mom—don't you already get up at the crack of dawn?"

"Yeah, but that's to do super fun things like change the baby's diaper, clean the kitchen, and fold three loads of laundry. Not something horrible like this."

"You actually enjoy doing those things?"

"Oh, God, no. I was just trying to impress upon you how much I'm not looking forward to this."

"Katie, it's a hike. It's walking. You walk every day of your life."

"But not by choice. I only do it because if I didn't, the kids would starve, the house would burn down, and there'd be nobody to get my copy of *US Weekly* out of the mailbox."

"You still read that trash?"

"Nothing makes me feel better than seeing pictures of celebrities when they look terrible. Knowing that people whose job it is to look beautiful can look that bad is the perfect self-esteem drug. That trash is what keeps me upright most days."

"Well, Katie Rodgers, a little exercise never hurt anyone."

"Other than people who have heart attacks, get hit by buses, or get attacked by grizzly bears."

"Yes, other than those people. That's an excellent caveat."

Katie rolled her eyes, and I grinned.

"C'mon, Katie. I haven't hiked along Moose River and up Moose Mountain in forever, and who better to share it with me than my best friend? You said you liked having me around, right?"

"I like having you around when we're drinking margaritas at the Taco House. If I knew you were going to make me exercise, I would never have forgiven you."

Stank reappeared with an old bucket of paint. "Here it is!" he announced, grinning ear to ear.

Katie peered at the can. "Any chance there's a very small person in there who might want to go hiking with Hope instead of me?"

Stank looked confused. "Um . . . no?"

"You have me at a loss," I said to Stank. "I'm not sure I know what that is."

He held up the paint can like he was showing off a trophy. "One gallon of premium Gentian Blue paint. Does that ring any bells?"

"Afraid not. What's so special about Gentian Blue paint?"

"You really don't recognize it, Hope? I've had this gallon of paint waiting for you since you left Hopeless. This is the color of the water tower."

At that, Katie cackled.

"You're kidding me," I said.

"I am not. After you got done painting the water tower for the second time, I figured it would be good to have an extra gallon of paint for you just in case. Look, we even marked it specially."

Stank turned the can around, and sure enough,

written in messy permanent marker were the words *Hope Walker*.

Katie cackled even louder.

"Am I supposed to be flattered or deeply offended?" I asked.

"I think a little of both," Katie said. "But think about it, Hope. All those celebrity designers have their own paint lines, but I'm betting those fixer-upper people don't handle paint for water towers. Think about the commercials you could run. 'Have you painted graffiti on your town's water tower? Well, my name's Hope Walker, and do I have the paint for you!'"

"I know Sheriff Kline's gone," Stank said, "but I was thinking, if you end up hating the new sheriff, this paint might just come in handy again."

Stank was, of course, referring to some . . . *unfortunate* incidents in my youth where I may or may not have gotten arrested for writing graffiti on the town water tower.

Katie smiled. "Oh, I don't think Hope hates the new sheriff." She poked me in the ribs.

Stank apparently caught her implication. "Oh? Oh! I see."

"*No,*" I said, waving my finger at both of them. "You don't see. You don't see anything at all. I sort of *do* hate the new sheriff."

"Right," Katie said.

"I do. I really do."

"Right," Stank said with a big wink. "Well, whatever the case, you are certainly free to take the paint home with you today—or I could just stick it in the back so it's here when you need it."

"I can think of somewhere else you could stick it," I said.

Stank laughed. "Now there's that feisty girl I remember. How about I just keep it in back then." He hollered down the hall. "April!"

When he got no response, he yelled louder. "April!"

A girl appeared. She wore blue jeans with holes in the knees, a brown bomber jacket, and white earbuds in her ears. Her head was covered in frizzy curly hair, and her light brown face was covered with a whole lot of attitude.

Stank held up the paint can. The girl rolled her eyes, grabbed it, spun around, and went back down the hallway without a word.

At that moment, the bell jingled on the front door, and a man entered. He wore khaki pants, a khaki shirt, and a hunter-green cap.

"Hey, Juan," Stank said. "You just missed Little Miss Sunshine."

"Oh, I'm afraid I got plenty of Miss Sunshine already this morning."

"So you're not back for a hug."

"I'm here for the orange spray paint."

Stank's eyes lit up with recognition. He grabbed a small cardboard box from behind the counter and handed it to the man. "Anything else?"

"Nope, that's it. Thanks, Stank."

"Oh, Juan, I'd like to introduce Katie Rodgers and, after a very long absence from these parts, Hope Walker."

Juan balanced the box in one arm while he shook

Katie's hand, then turned toward me with a questioning look.

"Hope's the one who solved those two murders," Stank said.

"Right! That's where I'd heard your name before." He held my hand a little too long, and he looked like he might want to say something more. But then he let go. "It was nice to meet you both. Thank you, Stank, as always."

As soon as the door shut, Stank clapped his hands and rubbed them together. "You didn't come in for water tower paint, and you didn't come in to ask me out on a date—though the answer is yes, by the way, for future reference. There must be something else you need."

"Was wondering if you had one of those filtered water bottles for hiking."

Stank looked at me like he was grossly offended, then pointed to the sign above his counter.

If you need it, we probably have it.
If we don't have it, we can probably steal it.
If we can't steal it, you probably don't need it.

HE WALKED over to the far wall, riffled through a cluttered mess of camping gear, and came out with a tall green water bottle. "One genuine water purifier and water bottle. You girls planning on doing some hiking today?"

"I haven't been up Moose Mountain in forever."

"And I couldn't get that root canal scheduled for today," Katie said. "So it's this instead."

Stank rang up the water bottle, then put it in a paper bag with my receipt. "Hard to imagine any granddaughter of Granny's needing a filtered water bottle. From what I remember, she drinks out of the Moose River like it's a fire hose."

"Sadly, I do not have the cast-iron stomach of my grandmother. I once saw her down an entire bottle of bourbon like it was a glass of orange juice . . . and then she spent the rest of the day chopping wood. That woman is tough."

Stank chuckled. "The way I hear it, you recently got hit by a car, then pulled yourself out of the hospital and solved two murders. That sounds pretty tough."

"I might be tough. I'm just not Granny tough. Anyway, thanks, Stank! Give my love to Cup."

Katie and I left Stank's and were walking to my car when a voice called out behind us.

"Excuse me? Hope?"

I turned around to find Juan standing on the sidewalk just outside Stank's, the cardboard box on the ground beside him, his hands in his pockets. He looked nervous.

"Hi, Juan," I said.

"You really solved those murders?"

"Um . . . yes."

"Don't be modest, Hope," Kate said. "You also falsely accused Mayor Jenkins in front of the whole town. Don't forget that!"

"I heard you were an investigative reporter back in Portland," Juan continued.

"You heard right. Juan, is something wrong?"

He looked around nervously. "Did you happen to see a teenage girl in Stank's?"

"Frizzy hair, holes in jeans, double helping of attitude . . .?"

"That's the one. Her name is April. She's my niece." He took a deep breath. "She's in trouble, and I need your help."

CHAPTER 2

We waited while an old farmer in overalls and a red seed cap ambled his way into Stank's, then Katie and I closed the distance between us and Juan.

"What kind of trouble is she in?"

He shook his head. "That's just it. I don't know. That's why I need your help."

"That's not exactly what I do."

"But you're an investigative reporter."

"I look into criminals and murders."

"And thieving foxes," Katie added.

"I don't have much experience with temperamental high school girls."

"Except that you *were* one," Katie pointed out.

"How do you know she's in trouble in the first place?" I asked Juan.

"April hasn't had an easy life. Her dad ran off when she was little, and her mother died young. I've been raising her ever since. We moved to Hopeless five years ago, and it's the best place we ever lived. I thought she was finally getting adjusted, finally fitting in . . . and then . . ."

"Then what?"

"End of last school year, things started to change. She just wasn't herself. She became withdrawn, distant. I asked her what was wrong, but she said it was nothing. And every time I tried to ask, she'd get angry. Like she just wanted to be left alone."

I felt for the guy, I did. It had to be difficult to raise a daughter on your own, especially when she wasn't even your daughter.

"Katie's right, Juan. I was a teenage girl once, believe it or not. And everything you're talking about . . . it sounds pretty normal."

Juan shook his head. "I know my niece. And you have to believe me, something is wrong."

"Have you looked into it yourself?"

"I asked some girls she used to hang around with—I thought they were her friends. But it got back to April, and she lost it on me. So I backed off. If I try looking into it again, she'll find out, and she'll withdraw even more. But you're a professional. It's your job to look into people . . . without them finding out."

"You want me to be your spy."

"If you help me out, you'd be my angel."

"This *really* isn't what I do."

"If I could pay you, I would."

"It's not about the money, Juan."

"I would be in your debt."

"She's a teenager. It's probably nothing."

"But what if it's something? What if it's something bad?"

I thought about it. The guy seemed really nice, and genuine in his concern for his niece. I had half a mind just to stride right into Stank's, yell at the girl, and get to the bottom of this here and now. But I knew that wouldn't work. I had been a teenage girl once, after all.

"Fine," I finally said. "I'll look into it. But I can't make any promises. And I need someplace to start. Sounds like her friends were a dead end. How about teachers? Is there any teacher she's close with?"

Juan's eyes lit up. "Mrs. Hamilton, her art teacher. I think the two of them are close." He grabbed my hand with both of his and shook it. "Thank you, Hope. Thank you so much."

"Like I said, no promises. But I'll do what I can."

Katie and I watched as Juan climbed into his little green pickup and drove down Main Street.

Then Katie put her arms around me and squeezed. "Who woulda thunk it? Hope Walker, big softie."

"You were the one practically begging me to help him."

"Because I'm a normal human being with a full range of emotions. You're the one who left her best friend for twelve years and hasn't been on one single date."

"I was sorta hoping we were done with the 'You've been gone twelve years' cracks."

"You thought we were done? Ha! You really *have* been gone a long time. Twelve years, to be exact."

"I think it's getting a little old."

"Not a chance. But you know what *is* getting a little old? My three children, who coincidentally you didn't even meet until two weeks ago . . . on account of you being gone for twelve years."

"I am not a big softie. The guy seemed desperate. And like you said, I know a thing or two about temperamental teenage girls. I'm sure it's nothing. I just want to ease his mind."

"But if it's something?"

"Then I guess we help her."

"We?"

"Oh, haven't you heard? I'm a superhero, and you're my trusty sidekick."

"I hate sidekicks."

"You know what you hate worse?"

"Non-alcoholic drinks? Making crafts with my kids? Small showers? Women who sell makeup at parties?"

"Hiking. Come on, princess. Moose Mountain awaits."

* * *

WE DROVE out Highway 15 past the spot where Jimmy and I had our accident so many years before. For twelve years, I'd tried to forget about that day, that spot. And in the two weeks I'd been back, I'd driven past it countless times. It was still hard. It still hurt.

But it was getting better.

We took a left on the little wooden bridge that led to the Crofton Bed-and-Breakfast. Since Patrick had died tragically two weeks before, the old cabin had sat empty.

Katie and I parked fifty yards down from the cabin right along the banks of the Moose River. The very same place where Granny and I would go when I was young so

I could wade into the river. The same place where Jimmy and I would go to have our picnics when I was older. I had a lot of memories here. But though I'd been back in Hopeless for two weeks, I had yet to come out here to enjoy the majestic wilderness that surrounded our weird little town.

Katie was already cursing when we got out of the car, but I wasn't listening. I had ears only for the sound of the Moose River, whooshing along in its rhythmic, hypnotic way. A sound from my dreams.

My good dreams.

I unscrewed the cap from my fancy new water bottle, knelt down beside the river, and filled it. I shook the water bottle, flipped up the little spout, and took a long, cool, satisfying drink. I could feel myself smiling. Really smiling.

But all Katie could do was shake her head. "You know they sell water in bottles," she said. "I could get you a twenty-four-pack for $2.99."

"It doesn't taste like this."

"It's water, Hope. It doesn't taste like anything."

"You ready to hike?"

"Do you like venereal diseases?"

"Excuse me?"

"I thought we were asking each other ridiculous questions."

"You're going to thank me, Katie Rodgers."

"I think we both know me well enough to know that's never going to happen. So instead of talking about it, let's just get this over with."

We hiked a trail along the Moose River for the next

fifteen minutes, then took a wooden bridge across the water. From there, the trail meandered into the foothills, and soon the trees swallowed us up. As wild as the old forest was on this side of Moose Mountain, it was hard to believe there could be cabins here—but there were. A couple dozen, hidden away like they'd become part of the landscape. That's how the people who lived on the mountain liked it.

And that's what made what Wilma Jenkins was trying to do with this side of the mountain even more infuriating.

We came to a steep spot in the trail. I grabbed hold of a small sapling, turned sideways with the terrain, and climbed my way up. Five feet later, I came to a plateau. I turned around to see Katie eying the sapling.

"I don't think Charlie Brown's Christmas tree is going to hold me."

I smiled. "It just needs a little love, that's all."

I reached down and held out my hand. Katie took it, and while I pulled, she dug in and climbed. Her face turned red as she hoisted herself up, and when she reached me, she let out a big breath.

"Isn't this fun?" I said.

"Hope, remember gym class, sophomore year, when Coach Bisbee put twelve minutes on the clock to see how many laps we could do around the field? And remember how he yelled at me the whole time to get my knees up because my run looked like a walk, and remember how I yelled back at him that my run looked like a walk because it *was* an effing walk?"

"I remember. You got to eat lunch with the principal the next day."

"Yeah, so all of that," she waved her arm in front of her face for effect, "all of that was more fun than hiking up this godforsaken hill."

"It's all in your perspective. First, you're with your best friend."

"Correction—I'm with the pain in the rear *formerly known as* my best friend . . . but who presently finds herself on probationary status." She smiled. "On account of the twelve-year absence."

"And there it is."

"Really, it doesn't get old."

"Second," I said, "you're not with your children."

Katie scratched her chin. "You actually do have a point there."

"Furthermore, Chris has to take care of them instead."

"And Celia did eat a couple of boxes of raisins last night."

"What's that mean?"

"It means pity the fool who has to change her diaper." Katie made a face. "You're making a solid case. However, I'm still walking up a very steep hill for what appears to be no good reason at all. Now, if you were to tell me that around the next corner was a giant bucket of Kentucky Fried Chicken, then we might have something to talk about."

"I've got something better."

I led the way up the slope for another thirty feet, then turned onto a narrow trail that jutted off to our left. After a short walk, the trees thinned out and we found ourselves standing atop a stone ledge. The drop-off was a few hundred feet, and at its bottom lay the Moose River and the surrounding valley.

Katie put her hands on her hips and looked from left to right. "I don't see a bucket of chicken."

"I know," I said, breathing in the crisp mountain air with my lungs and taking in the majestic sights with my eyes. "This view is so much better."

Katie raised an eyebrow again. "I feel like maybe you've never had Kentucky Fried Chicken before. It's really pretty spectacular."

"Katie Jo Rodgers!"

"Uh-oh, you're pulling out the middle name. This must be serious."

"It is. Now shut your mouth for once and just . . . I don't know . . . take this in. I mean, isn't this knock-you-in-the-side-of-the-head drop-dead beautiful?"

Katie laughed. "Yes, Hope, it is. I just like hassling you. I'm not sure it's worth how sore my butt is going to be tomorrow. But yes, it's pretty beautiful."

She and I stood there, letting the gentle breeze hit us in the face, while we took in my favorite place on earth. And something occurred to me. What happened to Jimmy and me . . . wow. That had to be some deep kind of painful to keep me away from this place—and from Katie—for so long.

Katie pointed down to our left. "Looks like the old cabin's got company."

She was right. Three vehicles had parked close to the cabin. One tiny figure got out of each vehicle.

"I don't believe it," Katie said.

"Don't believe what? Wait, can you actually see who those people are?"

"I got LASIK surgery last year. I've got super vision now. Hey, maybe that means you're the sidekick and I'm the superhero."

"Well, Supes, who is it?"

"It looks like it's a meeting of the Hope Walker Fan Club."

"What's that supposed to mean?"

"It means that's Gemima Clark and Mayor Wilma Jenkins. And from the looks of it, they're up to no good."

CHAPTER 3

Twenty-five minutes later, my very sweaty self arrived at the gravel driveway in front of the cabin. Wilma Jenkins, Gemima Clark, and a tall man in a three-piece suit with a brown leather briefcase were just exiting and walking out onto the front porch.

The man paid me no mind, but both Gemima and the mayor recoiled in disgust as soon as they saw me.

"What are *you* doing here?" Gemima said.

"I was about to ask you the same thing. Was there some sort of supervillain meeting I wasn't told about?"

Mayor Jenkins walked down the steps of the porch, her teeth showing. "Answer the question, Hope. What are you doing here?"

"Well, Your Majesty, in a free country like America, I thought I was permitted to come and go as I please. Without explaining myself to you."

Wilma Jenkins put both hands on her hips. "I'd call that ironic, considering how much you expect others to explain themselves to *you*."

"Come on, Mayor. You're still not bitter about that whole funeral thing, are you?"

"By 'funeral thing,' do you mean that time two weeks ago when you not only accused me of having an affair, you *also* accused me of killing two people—in front of the entire town? Is that what you mean? Because if so, then yes, I'm still bitter."

"If it makes you feel any better, you're the third mayor I've accused of double murder this month. In fact, I accused the pope of cattle rustling right before Christmas."

The man had come up alongside. "Is there some sort of problem?" he asked.

"Are you the secret head of this little crime syndicate?" I asked.

My question clearly confused him. He adjusted his glasses and pulled a business card from the inside of his suit coat. "My name is Malcolm Toomey, Esquire. I am not the head of any crime syndicate. I am a lawyer, and I have been appointed by the state of Idaho to act as the personal representative for the estate of Mr. Patrick Crofton."

I looked at Wilma, then back at Gemima.

"Ah, I get it. The vultures are swirling. But color me confused. Why would Patrick Crofton leave Wilma anything? He hated her."

Both Mayor Jenkins and Gemima were tight-lipped and looked . . . uncomfortable. They appeared to be trying to send some secret communique to Mr. Toomey.

He was not receiving their psychic messages. "Mr.

Crofton didn't leave anything to anybody," he said matter-of-factly. "That's the problem."

"Wait." I eyed both Gemima and the mayor. "Patrick didn't have a will?"

"No," Mr. Toomey said, oblivious to how much the three women around him hated one another.

"So he didn't leave Gemima everything?'

Gemima's face turned red.

"No, ma'am. Mr. Crofton didn't leave Miss Clark anything."

"Because he thought he was going to be *married* to me," Gemima snapped at the lawyer.

"I understand, Miss Clark. It's unfortunate, but as I've explained, an engagement carries no weight in inheritance law. All that matters is that Mr. Crofton had no will."

"Which shouldn't matter, should it?" Gemima said, getting heated. "He was going to marry me. It was his *wish* that everything go to me."

Mr. Toomey sighed. I could tell by his expression that he'd had this discussion with Gemima at least once already. "Without a will, the estate goes to probate, and the state has very clear laws about what must happen next."

"Well, Mr. Toomey," I said, "consider me a concerned citizen because I would very much like to hear what happens next."

"Of course. It's not a confidential process. We've officially opened the estate up for probate. Mr. Crofton's parents and his aunt are all deceased, and we can find no other living relatives."

"So . . . what does that mean?" I asked.

"It means that after the debts of his estate are settled, the remainder of the estate will go to the state of Idaho."

That's when I heard a terrible noise from behind me. Like some sort of wounded animal in great pain. I spun around to see Katie hunched over, hands pressed against her knees, wheezing to catch her breath.

"Don't . . . wait up . . . for me."

"You okay?" I asked.

"I'm pretty sure I had a stroke ten minutes ago. Why? Don't I *look* okay?"

"What's wrong with her?" Gemima asked.

"She's just upset there was no Kentucky Fried Chicken up on Moose Mountain today."

Mayor Jenkins looked like she was about to say something, then changed her mind. She took a breath and pursed her lips. "Mr. Toomey, we really should be on our way."

She and Gemima did another of those psychic looks, then the mayor steered Mr. Toomey past me and toward their cars.

That's when it hit me.

"If the estate is supposed to go back to the state, what are Wilma and Gemima doing here?"

Mr. Toomey stopped and turned. "The state has little interest in owning cabins and coffee shops. I have discretion to negotiate favorable terms on their behalf."

"Wait a second. Gemima and Mayor Jenkins are just going to carve up Patrick's estate without anybody else knowing about it?"

Wilma and Gemima gave each other another nervous look.

Mr. Toomey looked hurt. Like I'd just besmirched his reputation and that of all other probate lawyers. "We do not 'carve things up,' to use your words. My job is to follow the law. At all times. But if after the required six months, no relatives can be found, then yes, I have the discretion to make deals that are mutually beneficial to both the Crofton estate and the state of Idaho."

"Sounds kinda shady," I said.

"Sounds a *lot* shady." Katie was finally upright and next to me.

Mr. Toomey was about to say something more, but Mayor Jenkins held up a hand to stop him.

"Don't even bother, Mr. Toomey. Miss Walker has a habit of making unjustified accusations. I've been the target of her arrows before, and I'm sure I will be again."

"Wilma, if it means anything, I'm sorry I thought you killed two people. Satisfied?"

"Not remotely. You cost me a lot of money that day."

"Because I unmasked your skeezy real estate empire?"

"What I was doing was not, and *is* not, illegal."

"I didn't say 'illegal.' I said 'skeezy.'"

Gemima patted Wilma on the shoulder. "Forget it, Wilma. She's not worth it. Trust me, I've known Hope her entire life. She's never been worth much at all."

They gave each other another conspiratorial look. Then Wilma twisted her face into a smile. "Nice to see you again, Hope."

The three of them began walking to their cars.

Katie leaned in. "What the hell was that all about?"

I had a pretty good idea what it was all about. "Gemima doesn't really care about this old log cabin, does she?" I shouted.

That made all three of them stop.

"It's Mayor Jenkins who cares about the cabin. She cares about *all* the cabins." I'd remembered something. "But she cares about this cabin the most. I remember something Robert Lomax told me two weeks ago. That private meeting of the city board? He said it was about putting in a four-way intersection two miles outside of town on Highway 15. That intersection is an essential part of your plan to build Sawtooth Mountain Ski Resort. And you aim to do it right here, at Patrick's cabin."

The mayor's mouth twisted, and her nostrils flared.

"So, what deal have you two struck, Mayor?" I scratched my chin. "As long as Gemima doesn't challenge you for the cabin, are you just going to step aside and let her make a play for the Mercedes dealership and the coffee shop?"

Mr. Toomey adjusted his glasses. "Actually, according to our initial audit, the Mercedes dealership will need to be sold to cover the debts and taxes associated with the estate."

"Wow, Gemima," I said. "I'm sincerely surprised. All you get out of this is a measly coffee shop?"

"Turns out something is better than nothing," she said. "Unless your name is Hope Walker, when *nothing* is the best you're ever going to get. Leave it alone, Hope, and go take a shower. You stink. And yes, before you ask—worse than usual."

The mayor, Gemima, and Mr. Toomey finally made it into their cars.

I leaned in to Katie. "That was an odd thing to say, don't you think?"

"I'd say it was par for the course; the most *horrible person in the world* course."

"No, she said, 'Leave it alone.' In fact, that was the vibe I was getting the whole time. That they'd rather I just stay out of it. Or more exactly, they'd rather *everybody* stayed out of it."

"Well, of course. They don't want anyone to mess up their plans."

"And we've got six months to do just that."

"Hope . . . what are you playing at?"

Mr. Toomey's little gray sedan was already starting to crunch across the gravel. I sprinted over, jumped in front of it, held up my hands, and yelled "Stop." He looked at me like I was insane, but stopped and rolled down his window. Wilma and Gemima did the same.

"Are you mad?" Toomey said.

"You said you have the discretion to make deals that benefit both the Crofton estate and the state of Idaho."

"Yes."

"Well, here's the thing. Wilma Jenkins isn't the only one with a claim to that cabin. I wanted it long before her. Consider this my notification. When the six months are up, I plan on making an offer on this cabin."

"Hope!" Wilma shouted. "What you did at the funeral . . . that was stupid. But people can recover from stupid. You do this . . . and you declare *war*. People *don't* recover from that."

"Is that a threat? Katie, that sounded an awful lot like a threat."

Wilma growled. In normal life, she was a put-together, attractive woman. Charming, even. But at that moment, with her teeth showing, she didn't look attractive. She looked fierce.

"You stay out of our business," she said.

"Or what?"

"Or I'll a find a way into *your* business."

CHAPTER 4

"Well," Katie said as we re-entered Hopeless on the tourist side of town. "We've learned a lot today. For starters, beautiful scenic views are nowhere near as satisfying as Kentucky Fried Chicken."

"A point I disagree with."

"Thankfully, your vote doesn't count. On a related subject, hiking is every bit as terrible as I imagined."

"It wasn't that bad, Katie. You've given birth, right? I'm assuming *that's* a lot worse."

"It's worse for one terrible body-splitting minute. And then it's over. Sure, your bottom's sore for the next two months. But you get something good out of it."

"A fun and crazy boy who shoots strangers in the face with his dart gun."

"Exactly. With hiking, all you get is the sore bottom for two months."

"You forgot the very best part of today. Fresh mountain stream water." I shook my bottle in the air.

Katie snatched it away, tipped it back, and took a drink.

"Isn't it glorious?" I said.

"I'll let you in on a little secret. This clear liquid gold? I've got it set up at my house so it comes out of these magical things called faucets."

"You are a gigantic pain in my rear, Katie Rodgers."

She took another swig of water, then wiped her mouth. "And the other thing we learned today is that Hope Walker is a gigantic pain in the *mayor's* rear."

"She's crooked, Katie. You know it and I know it."

"She's also a very powerful woman. And if the funeral didn't do the trick, that little stunt back there sealed it. You, Hope Walker, have yourself an enemy."

"I thought Gemima was my enemy."

"Gemima's *our* enemy. Especially with what she did to those donuts."

"You still miss those little guys?"

Katie's eyes grew sad. "You have no idea. But Gemima's an enemy the same way Godzilla and King Kong are enemies. It's more . . . ancient and primal. With Wilma, I feel like you've gone out of your way to pick a fight."

"Are you crazy? Do you remember the part where I connected her to the Medola crime family?"

"What I remember is that you connected her to Tommy Medola's wife. That's not the same thing."

"Yes, Katie, it *is* the same thing. If Tommy Medola's wife is an investor in Wilma's Sawtooth Mountain Ski Resort, then Tommy Medola himself is an investor."

"If you say so."

"I do. And don't you see what she's trying to do? She's

going to bulldoze that cabin to make way for her precious four-way intersection, which will make way for her to bulldoze the entire side of that mountain."

"Hope, I know that once upon a time, that cabin meant a lot to you. But Jimmy's gone, and you haven't been here for twelve years."

"What are you saying?"

"I'm saying maybe Wilma's not the worst person in the world for having a different dream than you."

We stopped in front of Katie's house. Dominic was in the front yard, holding a hose and spraying it up at a second-floor window, where Lucy was looking down and sticking out her tongue.

"Looks like Chris has everything under control," I said.

"I bet you a hundred dollars he and the baby are lying on the couch watching *Craft Beer Countdown*."

"Huh?"

"Top twenty best-selling craft beers of the week."

"That's the dumbest thing I've ever heard in my life."

"Want to trade lives?" Katie said with an enormous fake smile.

"Tempting."

"Seriously, Hope. How could you even compete with Wilma in making an offer on the cabin? I heard Earl's paying you peanuts down at the *Hopeless News*."

"He's paying me less than peanuts, and he won't even cover my expenses."

"Then how? Did you hide a bunch of money away under your mattress I don't know about?"

"I'm not going to be working at the *News* for long. I've got feelers out for newspaper jobs all over the country."

Katie's fake smile was replaced with a look of hurt. "You're really going to move?" She threw her hands in the air. "So, why would you even want that old cabin?"

"First, I'm going to visit. As much as I can. And I'll need a place to stay. And second, I love that mountain and I don't want Wilma Jenkins to change it. As for the money, you're right. I don't have much. But I put five thousand dollars down on a fancy apartment in Portland, and I just talked to my lawyer yesterday and she felt really good about my chances of getting that money back."

Katie got out of the car, then leaned in through the open window. "Let me get this straight. Hope Walker and her five thousand bucks are going to go up against Wilma Jenkins and her entire real estate empire? Why don't I like those chances?"

"There's something else. Or actually, some*one* else."

"Granny."

"Yep. She was willing to back me once before. Maybe she'll do it again."

* * *

I FOUND Granny's legs sticking out from under her orange Ford Bronco in the crushed-rock driveway leading to her garage.

"Any chance you're stuck under there and I have to lift the truck off your chest?"

"I'd have better luck pushing this thing off all by myself."

"You calling me weak?"

"You've been doing sissy newspaper work for the last twelve years. I'm calling you soft."

"What are you doing under there, anyway?"

"I'm painting my nails. What the hell does it look like I'm doing? I'm fixing my truck. How was the hike?"

"I loved it. Katie hated it."

Granny snorted. "In other words, it was perfect."

"It's been too long."

"Yes, it has, granddaughter . . . but the important thing is, you're back."

I hesitated, not knowing how to approach the next part of the conversation.

"Uh-oh," Granny said.

"What do you mean, uh-oh?"

"You only go quiet like that when you've got something you need to talk about that you don't really want to talk about." Granny slid from under the Bronco and sat up on the little wheel cart. Her face was covered in black grease.

"I do not," I said.

"You do too. I'm too old for nonsense. Out with it."

"Fine. You were willing to do it before, so I thought maybe you'd do it again."

"Try sushi? Hell, no. I thought they were Jell-O shots that first time. That was a helluva cruel joke to pull on an old lady."

"I'm talking about the old cabin. My cabin. Would you be willing to help me buy it?"

Granny narrowed her eyes, rubbed her hand across her chin, took a breath, and shook her head. "No."

"What do you mean, no?"

She shrugged. "I mean no."

"Just like that?"

"Just like that."

She lay back down on her cart and scooted back under her old Bronco.

"Can I ask why?"

"Sure thing."

"Why?"

"Last time you asked, you were young. Didn't have a pot to piss in. You were in love. I don't know. Seemed right to help you."

"And now?"

"Now you're a grown-ass woman. You want to buy something that big, you buy it yourself."

"I can't believe you're being like this."

The cart rolled back until her face once again cleared the truck. She popped to her feet much faster than I thought was possible. Her jaw was tight. Her eyes were squinty.

This was Granny's "not messing around" face.

"I told you before. I understood why you left Hopeless. Didn't like it. Understood. But now that you're back, we need to get real. Something bad happened, so you left. Granddaughter, you need to realize something. Life is hard. Bad stuff happens all the time. You are a tough and stubborn girl. But sometimes, not tough enough."

"What are you talking about?"

"Sometimes when life gets too tough, you quit."

"I do not."

"After Jimmy, you did."

"That was different."

"No, Hope, it wasn't different. It was a pattern. You don't finish things."

"I was a very successful investigative reporter for twelve years. I think I know how to finish things."

"How about the biggest story of your career?"

"The Tommy Medola story? I finished it."

Granny's eyebrows went up. "Then why didn't I see it in the newspaper?"

"Because that chicken newspaper refused to run it."

"Sounds like something bad happened."

"Yes, it did."

"So, tell me. How much have you worked on that story since that chicken newspaper refused to run it?"

"What are you talking about? The story is dead."

Granny jabbed her finger into my chest so hard, I was certain I now knew what a bullet wound felt like. "The story's only dead if you let it die. This is your story. Not their story. You know what I want to see? I want to see a girl who is so tough and so stubborn and so pissed off, frankly, that she says 'Screw 'em. Screw all of 'em. I'm going to make this story so perfect, so sound, so unassailable with facts that they can't possibly *not* run the story.' And if you win a Wurlitzer to boot, that wouldn't be so bad either."

"It's a Pulitzer."

She winked. "I know."

I didn't say anything more. Neither did she. Her eyes changed from fierce to kind the way only Granny's could. She fished out her keychain and said, "Follow me."

We walked into her garage. To a large wooden wardrobe in the back, its doors padlocked.

"What's this?"

She undid the padlock, handed me the little key, and opened the doors. "Bess and I call this 'Hope's Closet of Unfinished Stuff.'"

"You can't be serious."

"Have a look for yourself."

Under Granny's watchful gaze, I looked through old memories of my life. Businesses, projects, plans that I'd started, but never finished. I guess I'd always dismissed those start-and-stop dreams as a feature of my youth. That somehow I'd left all that behind and grown up. But maybe . . . there *was* a pattern.

"You're right, Granny. As much as it pains me to admit it, you're right."

"I couldn't care less about being right, Hope. The question is, what are you going to do about it?"

"I'm not going to stop investigating Tommy Medola. In fact, our good mayor has given me a fresh new source of inquiry."

"Good."

"And you're right about the other thing. I'm a grown-ass woman, and I need to make my own money. As soon as I find a good job, I will. But for now, Earl's paying me practically nothing. Which means . . . if you happen to know how I could earn some money, I'd be willing to listen."

Granny smiled. "That's what I like to hear. And it turns out, there's one more project that belongs in Hope's Closet of Unfinished Stuff . . . but it was too big to fit inside the closet." She led me back out of the garage and looked up at the side of her two-story farmhouse. The old paint was peeling all over. "This is your biggest unfinished project. I was curious about it a few days ago, so I looked at one of my journals, and wouldn't you know, we're coming up on a very auspicious date."

"Granny, what are you talking about?"

"Once upon a time, you were going to paint this house for me—for a hundred and seventy-five dollars. When you were nineteen, that wasn't anything to sneeze at. You started, then you stopped, then you started, then you stopped. One day, I told you you'd never get this painted. You yelled at me and said you would. Now, I don't know why I chose this number, but I remember it. I said if I gave you thirteen *years*, you still wouldn't finish this house. Well, what do you know—next Saturday will mark thirteen years from that date. And guess what? The house still hasn't been painted."

I couldn't believe what I was hearing. "You want me to paint this entire house . . . for a hundred and seventy-five dollars . . . by next Saturday? You're insane."

"So, you're not going to follow through on your commitment?"

"I get the lesson you're trying to teach me, Granny, I really do. But to paint this entire house? And to paint it for a hundred and seventy-five bucks? No way."

Granny shrugged. "So much for commitments."

"It's not that. It's just . . . that kind of money is a drop in the ocean of what I'll need to buy that cabin."

"Oh, I see. So money's suddenly growing out of your keister?"

"Not exactly. But my lawyer is confident that I'm going to recover my five-thousand-dollar deposit for my apartment in Portland. And five thousand is a heckuva lot more than one seventy-five."

"Well, okay then. Sounds like you've got a plan. But the house and one seventy-five are waiting for you if you need them."

CHAPTER 5

After talking with Granny, I decided to check in with my lawyer.

"Hi, Margaret. It's Hope."

"Oh, Hope. I guess I'm glad you called."

"I was wondering if you had an update for me about my deposit."

"Actually, yes. I know I told you yesterday I thought everything would work out, but . . ."

My heart dropped into my stomach. "But?"

The "but" was that the apartment complex had done a little research on me and determined that I was out of a job. Which meant I couldn't afford to put up much of a legal battle. Which meant they really had no reason to take any of my lawyer's threats seriously.

They wouldn't be giving me my deposit back after all.

That five thousand dollars represented the sum total of my life savings. Of course, that was past tense.

Which meant I wasn't just hurting for money.

I *had* no money.

Which explained why twenty minutes after telling Granny I would never paint her house, I was twenty feet up a ladder with a paint scraper in my hand, very much hoping I was not about to fall to my death.

"You're not doing it right," Granny shouted at me from below.

Her presence caught me by surprise, and I felt myself slip. The ladder rattled back and forth. I steadied myself against a shutter of the old house before carefully looking down.

Granny had her hand to her chin like she was inspecting my work. "Now you're *really* not doing it right," she said.

"Do you have anything helpful to say?"

"I really doubt you'll be able to get this done by next Saturday."

"How is that helpful?"

Granny just shrugged.

I had just started to go back to work when Granny spoke again.

"Your rump's bigger than it used to be."

"Granny!"

"I'm just saying. You know Cheetos will do that to a girl."

"I don't eat Cheetos."

Granny raised both eyebrows.

"Okay, I don't eat very *many* Cheetos. Just as a garnish . . . not as a food group. And this still isn't helpful."

"Sure it is. Now you know that when you fall off that ladder, you need to make sure to land on that big old caboose."

"Okay, Granny. Enough with the butt cracks."

I realized my error as soon as the unfortunate turn of phrase left my mouth.

Granny's chuckle turned into uproarious laughter. "Bess!" she yelled toward the house. "Bess! You ought to hear what Hope just said."

There she was. My granny. A wrinkly old woman wearing a blue Boise State Football sweatshirt. All the wisdom of an eighty-year-old woman and all the maturity of a thirteen-year-old boy.

Gripping the ladder with one hand, I moved my other hand behind me and grabbed hold of the rump in question. It was possible that my less-than-stellar diet had added a bit of girth down there. But then I had another thought. I snatched my hand back and examined it closely.

"That's it!" I said to myself. "My hand is just smaller than it used to be."

Believe it or not, that actually helped. I took my magically shrinking hand, adjusted my grip on Granny's putty knife, and went back to the tiresome business of scraping old paint off Granny's even older house. It was mind-numbing, tedious work, the kind of work that I'd hated to do my entire life.

It reminded me of the time Granny ran for president of the school board and made me lick a few hundred envelopes for a mailer she was doing. I got so tired of all that licking that I started making Granny's old cat, Perdy, lick them instead. And my plan worked pretty great . . . until Perdy started retching all over the place like she'd been poisoned. Because, well . . . she had been poisoned.

Perdy was eventually fine, but as my punishment for nearly killing the cat with United States Postal Service adhesive, Granny made me dust the entire house, weed the flower garden, and alphabetize every single book in the house.

If Granny's goal was to make sure I would never, ever again poison the family cat, her punishment worked brilliantly. If, on the other hand, she expected me to fall in love with tedium, she had miscalculated.

And yet here I was, scraping away peeling old paint on a huge old house on a rickety old ladder. I was engulfed in a sea of tedium.

And I hated it.

I had raised up onto my tippy-toes to reach a spot above the windows when I heard a delighted high-pitched squeal. I knew that squeal.

Oh, no. Please, no.

I looked down to see Katie on the lawn, setting up a camping chair while her two oldest children were pulling her baby in an old red wagon.

"What in the hell are you doing here?" I shouted. "I thought you'd be soaking in an ice bath by now."

"And miss *this*? Nope. Granny called. Said something about butt cracks. Figured after what you put me through this morning, the kiddos and I needed to get over here as quickly as possible."

"What for?"

Katie leaned back in the lawn chair, kicked up her feet, and donned a pair of dark sunglasses. "Butt patrol," she said with a wide smile.

"I really hate you, Katie Rodgers."

"I know you do. But what's a girl to do?"

"Help?"

"Nah. I'd rather watch you, make a bunch of smart-aleck comments, and let my son use you for dart gun practice."

"Did you seriously come over here just to watch me work?"

She shrugged. "It wasn't my first choice, but our TV in the bedroom broke after I threw a brush at it."

"Why'd you throw a brush at your TV?"

"Because that idiot Louis chose Faith instead of Amber."

"What are you talking about?"

"The latest season of *Bachelor in Buffalo*."

"There's a *Bachelor in Buffalo*? As in Buffalo, New York?"

"Yeah. I DVR'd the episode from late last night and when I returned from our hike from hell, I watched it. You'd think *Bachelor in Paradise* would be the best, getting to see romance in the middle of white sandy beaches and leafy jungles, but nothing says true love like trying to navigate a Putt-Putt date in twenty-below wind chill and fourteen inches of lake-effect snow. But that idiot Louis couldn't see that Faith is a backstabbing gold digger, so now we're down to one TV and Chris is watching a documentary on craft beers. I'm not kidding, Hope—I'm literally going to kill myself If I have to watch another documentary on craft beers."

"There's more than one?"

"Oh, my God, yes. There's a whole show on Netflix called *Crafties: The Heroic Men Who Shaped an Industry*. He made me watch the entire first season with him. He said I owed him after I lied to him about the credit card debacle."

"So, now you're even?"

"I'm lounging in an old lady's backyard trying to figure out just how big my old best friend's butt has gotten. Does that sound like *even* to you?"

"Let me get this straight. I'm on top of a ladder that could collapse at any moment, scraping paint and who-knows-what chemicals off a hundred-year-old house while my granny is apparently selling tickets for people to come and make fun of my posterior… and *you're* the one I'm supposed to feel sorry for?"

"Wow. You summarized that quite nicely." Katie looked over at her kids. "Dominic! Time to shoot Aunt Hopie in the you-know-whatie!"

The little terrorist grabbed his Nerf blaster out of the wagon and held it at the ready. I considered throwing the putty knife at the animal, but his life was saved by my phone buzzing in my pocket. My elbow looped around the top rung, and I fished it out. It was a local Hopeless number, but I couldn't place it.

"Hello?" I said.

"Hope, it's Earl Denton. We've got an emergency, and I need you at the office five minutes ago."

"What for?"

"The biggest story of the year."

CHAPTER 6

I pulled up to the curb, jumped out of my car, and sprinted into the offices of the *Hopeless News*. It wasn't every day one got to cover the biggest story of the year. And as excited as Earl had sounded on the phone, I was more than a little curious to figure out what this story was all about.

I found him in his office, baseball cap on his head, a much-too-large Hawaiian shirt hanging off his shoulders. He was zipping up a suitcase on the floor, but looked up when he heard me enter.

He frowned. "You look like crap."

"Nice to see you too, Earl."

"I'm serious. Why do you look like that?"

"I was painting Granny's house."

"Why?"

"Because I need money."

"Why?"

"Because you pay me less than peanuts, and you refuse to cover my expenses."

Earl rolled his eyes as he walked to his desk. "Not this again."

"Yes, Earl, this again. I drove three hundred miles last week chasing that story about the 'wild dog' that was eating chickens all around Hopeless."

"And I sincerely appreciate you cracking the Case of the Thieving Fox. Our readership appreciated it."

"But Earl, I don't have a magic car that runs on magic gasoline. I have a real car that runs on regular unleaded . . . which I can't pay for unless you pay my expenses. That's how this works."

"No, that's how things worked in Portland. This ain't no fancy town, it ain't no fancy newspaper, and I sure as hell ain't no fancy boss."

"So you're really not going to pay for my expenses."

"I'm going to do better. I'm going to give you the same advice my boss gave me when I was a young man. He said, 'Earl, the best way to deal with expenses is not to have any.'"

"Your boss was an idiot."

"My boss was my father."

"I meant 'idiot' in the best kind of way. Like they do in France. It's a great compliment, really. Okay, Earl, stop keeping me in suspense. What's the biggest story of the year, and what does it have to do with your suitcase and Hawaiian shirt?"

"Camilla and I are going on a fancy cruise. She figures with you here to do the reporting, it was time I took her on a proper vacation."

"Okay. But you said there was a big story."

Earl smiled and raised his finger. "There is. I was so busy getting ready that I completely forgot what today is."

"It's Saturday."

"Not just Saturday. It's the third Saturday of September."

"I'm supposed to do a story about the third Saturday of September?"

"You're supposed to do a story on the most important social event of the entire year—Mrs. Thorndale's big party!"

I pressed my eyes shut. "You said you had an emergency. And I come to find out it's just a social gathering for a rich old lady?"

"Oh, so you remember the Thorndales."

"Kind of. Katie and I TP'd their pool house in high school."

"Ha! Did they catch you?"

"Their security guard did. I said my name was Gemima Clark, then I kicked him and we ran away. Look, I don't really have to go to this thing, do I?"

"Yes, you do. Mrs. Thorndale is a snooty old lady, but she's a *rich* snooty old lady, and her generous yearly donation helps keep the *Hopeless News* in business. One of the strings attached to that donation is that we devote the front page of the paper to her big party."

"I'm hoping this is all a cruel joke."

"And I was hoping you wouldn't look so terrible."

"Why do you keep saying that?"

Earl checked his watch. "Because you've got to be at the party in five minutes."

"What? Earl! I can't go looking like this."

"Hence why I keep mentioning how terrible you look."

I grabbed my hair. "I've got to shower, do my hair and makeup, put on some decent clothes . . ."

"And by that time, you'll miss half the party, and Mrs. Thorndale will conveniently forget to send me her donation for next year. Nope, you'll have to go as is. But don't worry—I've got just the thing to fix this."

Earl bent over, rummaged through a big cardboard box, and pulled out something large, neon yellow, and hideous.

"What . . . *is* that?"

He unfolded it, threw it over my head, and pulled it down onto my shoulders. "This, Hope Walker, is an official *Hopeless News* reporter's safety vest. It was a gift from the county roads department a few years ago. You wear this, and nobody will care about the rest of you."

"Because it makes me look like a lighthouse."

Earl looked at his watch. "Two minutes, Hope. Or Isabelle Thorndale is going to be one very *angry* snooty old rich lady." He grabbed me by the shoulders, turned me around, and ushered me out of the building. "Remember—lots of pictures. Lots of names. You hear anything that sounds pretentious or bombastic—like Mrs. Thorndale talking about their yacht in Mazatlán or their breeder poodles from Surrey—write it down. She loves that stuff."

I climbed into my car, feeling very much like I'd just been ambushed, and rolled down my window. "Mrs. Thorndale's party wasn't exactly what I had in mind when I decided to become an investigative reporter."

Earl smiled and tapped the top of my car. "Like I keep telling you, Dorothy, you're not in Portland anymore."

* * *

The Thorndales' estate sat along Frampton Road on the slope side of Moose Mountain. Old sugar maples lined both sides of the stately street, their branches forming a leafy green canopy overhead. A black wrought-iron fence protected the Thorndale estate from the rest of Hopeless, and inside that fence, packing a lush green lawn, were a great deal of people wearing fancy suits, pretty dresses, and elegant hats.

A teenaged boy in a burgundy coat directed me to the parking area—another grassy area at the far end of the estate, with orange spray paint marking out spaces. I took one last look in the rearview mirror before getting out of my car. My makeup from the day before still half clung to my face. My hair stood up and out at odd angles. I was wearing a giant neon sign, and one whiff of my armpit told me that I should definitely see the inside of a shower at some point in the very near future.

Official *Hopeless News* vest or not, this simply wouldn't do.

I rummaged around in my back seat and found an old ball cap. I pulled my hair into a ponytail and slid the hat on. The look didn't exactly scream "fancy party," but it was a definite improvement. Then I saw the evergreen-scented cardboard tree that hung from my mirror, and I had a brilliant, if mildly disgusting, idea.

I grabbed the little evergreen tree and rubbed it under both arms. Then I dabbed it against both sides of my neck for good measure.

I looked at the woman in the mirror who'd just used a

car freshener for a Marine Corps shower. "Who you looking at?" I growled.

I hopped out of the car and saw a parking attendant smiling at me. Although he had changed into the same burgundy sport coat as the boy by the front gate, I recognized Juan immediately. "You clean up good," I said.

He glanced at my bright yellow vest and was obviously uncertain what compliment he could pay me in return. He wisely moved on. "Have you learned anything about my niece yet?"

"You did only ask me about her a few hours ago . . . so, no."

He winked. "I was kidding." He shrugged. "Well, mostly. Enjoy the party."

As I hustled along the sidewalk, I heard the crackle of a loudspeaker. At the front gate, the teenage boy gave me a weird look.

"Dude, that vest makes you look like a night-light."

I saw he had a name tag. "Carl," I said, "do you by chance have a girlfriend?"

His shoulders slumped. "No."

"It might have something to do with calling women 'dude.' Just an observation."

I made my way to the big front lawn, where people wearing blue blazers and long dresses were holding drinks. Somebody was speaking at a microphone set up on a temporary stage.

A tough-looking older man saw me and frowned. He too was wearing a burgundy sport coat. And he was walking my way. "Excuse me. Are you lost?"

"This is Mrs. Thorndale's party, right?"

He nodded.

"Then I am not lost."

He gestured to the crowd. "As you can see, ma'am, there is a dress code, and as *I* can see . . . you are dressed like a lampshade."

"First 'night-light' and now 'lampshade'? You and Carl should really take this act on the road."

The man pursed his lips. He was not amused.

"Listen," I said. "I'm here with the *Hopeless News* to cover the party."

"You are not Earl Denton."

"You probably don't have a girlfriend either, do you?"

"Excuse me?"

"I'm sorry. I just need to cover the party for Mrs. Thorndale, okay?"

He looked like he was going to let me go. Then suddenly his expression changed. His mouth opened. His eyes widened. His eyebrows craned downward.

"You!" he said, his voice shaking.

"Me what?"

He stepped closer. "I remember you," he growled. "I'd never forget you. It's you. It's you!"

"It's me what?"

"It must have been thirteen . . . maybe fourteen years ago. I was patrolling the grounds when I caught two kids TP'ing the house. I caught one of them. Until she kicked me. Kicked me where it hurt. I swore that night that someday, I would find you. Well, young lady, someday is finally here."

CHAPTER 7

The man looked like he wanted to kill me, but I figured I could defuse the situation with my usual charm.

"You're the guy I kicked in the yoohoo?"

His face turned an even deeper shade of red.

"Listen." I glanced at his name tag. Mortimer Snoot, Head of Security. "Mr. Snoot, I was sixteen and you just caught me TP'ing a house, and I was more concerned about the sheriff than you, so . . . yes, I kicked you. I'm really sorry. Do you think we could just move on? I know I have."

One look at his face told me that Mr. Mortimer Snoot, Head of Security, was *not* ready to move on. Not by a long shot.

"You told me your name was Gemima Clark," he said. "Well, I tracked Ms. Clark down, and imagine my surprise when she wasn't you."

"Surprise? Did you really expect me to tell the truth? Have you ever met a sixteen-year-old kid before?"

Mortimer Snoot growled yet again.

"Isn't it unhealthy how nobody in this town can forget the bad things I once did to them? Okay, would you believe me If I told you that I am honestly sorry for doing that to you, and if it makes you feel better, I will pinky promise that I will never, ever, ever kick you in the yoohoo ever again?"

He grabbed me by the shoulder. "No, it would not." Little bits of spittle hit me in the face. "It would make me feel better to throw you out of this party on your ear."

"Hey!" I said as he started pulling me toward the gate. "I've got a job to do! I have to cover this party for the *Hopeless News*!"

He was full-on dragging me now, and I wondered if I might have to fall back on my old tricks. It had been a while since I'd given a man a proper kick to the giblets, but I figured I still had it in me.

"I don't care what you have to do," he snapped. "I'm throwing you out."

I started to twist my body and cock back my foot.

"I don't believe you *are* throwing her out," said a calm and sturdy voice from behind me.

Mr. Snoot looked past me and stopped. "Um, er . . . hello, Sheriff."

Sheriff?

I spun around to see the sheriff of Hopeless, Idaho, in the flesh.

This was not the sheriff I had hated in my youth. That sheriff was Ed Kline, and after I solved his recent murder, I learned that he had been a better guy than I had ever imagined. But the man before me now was Sheriff Kline's replacement. Alex Kramer. Former homicide detective for the state police. And on the day I confronted Ed Kline's killer, he was the man who sort of saved my life.

I hadn't seen him much since then. I'd been busy getting settled into my new but hopefully only temporary life. And he, no doubt, had been busy with his job as the new sheriff of our weird little town.

Yet here he was, coming to my aid once again.

Alex was tall and lean, with wide shoulders and a square jaw. He was handsome in the nauseating way daytime soap opera stars are. But his eyes . . . they made me stop and lose my breath. Unnaturally green. And fierce. The kind of eyes that made me want to know more.

Still, as good as Alex looked—and he did look good—something wasn't quite right. It was the clothes. His new official sheriff clothes. Black combat boots, dark khaki pants, and a chocolate brown shirt with a dark tie and a gold star. Somehow they made him look just like Sheriff Ed Kline.

Hot Alex Kramer morphs into grumpy old dead Sheriff Kline.

Weird.

"Just what exactly is going on here?" he asked.

"I'm throwing this woman out of the party."

"What for?"

"She assaulted me."

Sheriff Kramer flashed just a hint of a smile. "Sounds about right. What specifically did she do?"

"She kicked me in . . . well, she kicked me in the place that shall not be mentioned."

Alex's eyebrows arched. "I see." He rubbed his jaw. "That actually might be a pretty good reason to throw her out."

I scowled. "Ask him *when* I kicked him in the place that shall not be mentioned."

"Mr. Snoot?"

"I don't see how that's relevant."

Alex waited silently.

"Fine. It happened thirteen years ago." Snoot pointed toward the pool. "Right over there. I had just nabbed her for TP'ing the pool house."

"Did you just say 'thirteen years'?"

"And two months. I remember it well. Mortimer Snoot doesn't forget."

"Okay, two things. First, your name is actually Mortimer Snoot? And second, the statute of limitations for kicking someone in the place that shall not be mentioned is seven years. I just looked it up the other day. I'm sorry, Mr. Snoot, but you've got no cause. I'd suggest you let her go."

It was apparent by his grip around my shoulder that Mr. Snoot had no intention of letting me go.

"I can remove anybody from this estate I choose. As the head of security, that is my purview."

Alex took an intimidating step toward us. "And *I* can remove anybody from this *town* that I choose. As the head of security for Hopeless, that is *my* purview." He narrowed his eyes, and Mr. Snoot let go of my shoulder.

His eyes filled with rage. "I'm not finished with you, young lady."

"It was just a kick, man. I mean, can't you let it go?"

"I had to ice the area that shall not be mentioned for an entire week. So no, I can most definitely not 'let it go.'"

He shot me one more angry look before releasing a hot, nasty breath from his nose and storming off.

And that left me alone with Sheriff Kramer.

"Thanks," I said.

"Seems I'm keeping busy saving your life all the time."

"Oh, you just saved my life?"

"You really kicked him in the . . . um . . .?"

"Merry giblets? Oh, yeah. Hard. Really hard. I could hear the poor guy screaming as I jumped the fence. Katie and I laughed about it the whole way home. I actually felt bad about it. But now that I've met Mr. Snoot, I don't feel bad anymore." I took a step back. "So, look at you all sheriffed up."

"Yeah, well, I told Katie to order me a sheriff's uniform, and this is what she got."

"You look kind of like Eric Estrada from *CHiPs*. If he was wearing a cowboy hat."

"I think that's an insult. Right?"

"Not at all. I bet Eric Estrada was a super cool guy in 1978."

He laughed. "I'm certain *that's* an insult."

For a moment, I forgot about his stiff and dorky sheriff clothes and just focused on his face. My heart beat faster, and I felt my breath grow shallow.

I sure wish he didn't have that effect on me.

"So, what's with *your* outfit?" he said, smiling. "Let me guess . . . you're performing a light show for the afternoon entertainment? Fireworks display?"

"Okay, wisenheimer, that's enough."

He snapped his fingers. "I've got it. If the sun burns out this afternoon, you're the substitute."

"If you must know, this is the official reporter's vest for the *Hopeless News*. And as much as I would prefer to be on top of a 1965 Sears & Roebuck ladder painting my granny's house, I am instead here, covering the greatest social event of the year."

Alex looked out over the vast lawn and all the people milling about. "You think it's really that bad?"

"I'm sure it's worse. But Earl Denton wants me to cover it, so I'm going to cover the hell out of it. And you?"

"Mayor Jenkins told me that the town expects the sheriff to show up at these things and meet people. And if Mr. Snoot's an indicator, it should be a super fun party. Hey, you figure a reporter at the *Hopeless News* is allowed to drink at an event like this?"

"I figure it would be criminal if I *didn't* drink at an event like this. Is a sheriff allowed to drink on duty?"

"It's Saturday. I don't think a beer or two could hurt."

We walked together toward an outdoor bar. "So, has our little town quieted down at all since your initial reception?" I asked.

"Now it's *our* town?" he said. "Word on the street is that your days in Hopeless are numbered. That you're just waiting for a better offer to come along."

"That's no offense to Hopeless. It's just that I'm an investigative reporter, and the big cities have most of the investigations."

"Except for the occasional double murder."

"Except for that."

The conversation stalled out there. It seemed like he was going to say something, but didn't. Then I thought about saying something, but didn't. Being with him made me a little nervous. And that made me think I'd better come up with something funny to say, and quick. But just as I was coming up with something, the worst thing in the world happened.

Mayor Jenkins and Gemima Clark walked up. They both took one look at me and my ridiculous outfit, then turned to each other and laughed.

Gemima hooked her arm through Sheriff Kramer's, and Wilma said, "You're coming with us, Sheriff. It's time you met your town."

And just like that, they ushered Alex away. I'd like to say "*poor* Alex," but I wasn't so certain he hated the attention.

And really, who was I kidding? I was in no condition to compete with Gemima and her flawless figure, or Wilma and her real estate empire. So instead of competing, I would do what I was good at. Because what I *could* do—and I could do this as well as anyone—was drink at the inappropriate time.

The bar was staffed by a thin woman with short hair and the gaunt, wrinkly face of a lifelong smoker. As I walked up, she shook her head. "We're not supposed to serve the help."

"The help?" I said.

She shrugged. "Hey, I've got nothing against chicks working construction, but rules are rules." She leaned over the bar and lowered her voice. "You never heard this from me, but extra rolls and desserts usually get set outside the kitchen in back. So if you can hold your powder, you might get lucky."

"I'm not a construction worker."

"Oh. Are you the token broad they keep on the crew who holds the sign telling people to slow down?"

"Are you actually a woman?"

"Last time I checked."

"You may want to check again."

She looked mildly offended.

"Don't mind Mrs. Scratchett here," said a voice on my left.

I turned to see a handsome woman in her early forties. She had stylish brown hair, dangly hoop earrings, and an impossibly low-cut blue dress.

"She's a good maid and makes a helluva Bloody Mary, but her people skills leave a little to be desired." The woman looked sternly at the bartender. "Mrs. Scratchett, this woman is *not* a construction worker." She grabbed my yellow vest and pointed. "She's a reporter with the *Hopeless News*."

"I'm sorry, ma'am. It's just that Pimsey got on my case last year when I let the ice sculptor do Jell-O shots."

"After all these years, you're still scared of Pimsey?"

"No, I ain't scared of that stuffed shirt. I just prefer not to have to talk to him more than necessary."

"Speaking of Pimsey, I haven't seen him, and Mother's getting nervous."

Scratchett gave her a look. "You don't know about last night?"

"What happened?"

"Your mother and Pimsey happened."

"And now?"

"I haven't seen Pimsey all morning."

"You think he flew the coop?"

"I am not my butler's keeper. Your guess is as good as mine."

"Crap. Mother's gonna freak." The woman shook her head and chewed on her lower lip.

Then she looked at me and forced a smile. "Where are my manners?" She shot out her hand, and I took it. "Valerie Thorndale."

"Hope Walker."

"I wish I could talk, but there's a matter that needs my attention. Mrs. Scratchett. get Ms. Walker here whatever she wants to drink. Time to go see Mother."

"Actually," I said, "your mother is who I need to see. I've got to write this article, and to be candid, seeing as I'm not really dressed for this party, I'm not sure I can do that by mingling. I think it would be better if I just talked to her directly about what she'd like me to write."

"Have you met my mother? She's not the easiest person to talk to."

"I'm a big girl reporter. Don't worry, I can handle your mother."

"Well, that's where you're wrong. I've never ever seen anyone 'handle' my mother. I can promise you only one thing." Valerie made the kind of face people make when they have indigestion. "Whatever's about to happen, it won't be pleasant."

CHAPTER 8

As we walked across the lawn, Valerie smiled and waved like she'd been handling crowds like this her entire life.

"So, you're a Thorndale?" I asked.

"Ouch."

"I didn't mean it like that."

"Yes, you did. And it's okay—I'm used to it. Plus, I'd expect nothing less than honesty from Granny's kin."

"You know Granny?"

"Everyone knows Granny. And I remember seeing you in the Library when you were little. But I was gone from Hopeless by the time you grew up, and then when I returned . . . I guess it was your turn to fly the coop."

"What brought you back?"

She winked. "I only come back on a part-time basis. And when I do?" She spun around with her arms extended. "It's for all this, of course. In case it's not nauseatingly clear, my mother is rich. And I figure she's bound to die one of these days. If I don't at least pretend to like her, there's no way she'll leave me anything."

"That's cold."

"Someday, if you get enough wine in me, maybe I'll tell you about the Thorndale Challenge."

"Intriguing."

"More like humiliating. Anyway, have you ever actually met my mother?"

"I TP'd her pool house in high school. Does that count?"

Valerie's eyes widened. "You're not the one who kicked old Snoot in the family jewels, are you?"

I jabbed a thumb proudly at my chest. "In the flesh."

Her mouth widened into a bright, happy smile. "I detest that man. You know, I believe you and I might just become friends."

"Might?"

"Let's see how you do with my mother first. Remember, I'm still working on that inheritance."

"What can you tell me about her?"

"Other than she's a nightmare?" She clucked her tongue. "Let me see. She loves money. She hates people. And more than anything else, she loves throwing this party to show all the people she hates how much money she has. No, wait—there is *one* thing she loves more than this party. Her Knutsen."

"What the hell's a Knutsen?"

Valerie laughed. And then she saw that I was serious. "Oh, you really don't know?"

"I don't have a clue."

"You haven't been around much."

"Valerie!" a harsh voice shrieked.

I turned around to find an older woman glaring at me with fiery eyes and a gaunt, lifeless face somehow kept alive by a copious amount of makeup. Her silver hair had streaks of black, matching her black rhinestone dress and long black-and-white scarf. She was giving off a serious Cruella de Vil vibe. This was definitely a woman who was marching into the last years of her life. She was doing it with lots of money. And she was not doing it gracefully.

This was Isabelle Thorndale.

"What . . . *are* you?" she asked with as much contempt as a human being could manage.

Since I was quite certain a bucket of water might melt the woman, I figured I could ask her the same thing. But the rare and seldom-used tactful part of my personality took over.

"My name is Hope Walker. Earl Denton sent me to cover your party for the *Hopeless News*."

She recoiled. "Earl sent someone else?" She looked at her daughter. "Did you know about this?"

"As a matter of fact, Mother, I did," Valerie said. "And before you say anything, I ran a complete background check, and she's clear. Except for the violent offender registry—but honestly, they *make* you sign up for that. And her drug test came back free and clear. Except for the weed, but who am I kidding? She was living in Portland."

Isabelle Thorndale looked at her daughter for a long moment. "I know you *think* you're being funny . . ." She trained her dragon eyes on me. "So, I'm stuck with you?"

"I'm afraid so."

She shook her head and growled. "Well, don't mess

this up. I give that newspaper a sizeable donation each year, and it's not because I care about news, freedom of the press, or any of that nonsense."

"Mother, Scratchett tells me that you and Pimsey got into a bit of a tiff last night."

Isabelle Thorndale rolled her eyes like a thirteen-year-old girl. "Pimsey's a buffoon."

"He's a proper English butler, Mother. I'd hardly call him a buffoon."

"Don't let the haughty accent fool you. He's a below-average butler and an *above*-average buffoon."

"What happened?"

"That's between me and the buffoon."

Valerie shook her head. "Not anymore."

"What's that supposed to mean?"

"It means I haven't seen him anywhere."

The elder Thorndale's eyes twitched nervously. "I haven't either. Like I said, below-average butler. He's probably sulking in his room. You'd better go get him. We're about to do the unveiling."

"I don't think he's sulking, Mother. Neither does Scratchett. I think he's gone."

Isabelle's eyebrows arched. "He wouldn't! Not today of all days."

"Don't act like it's the first time he's left."

"But never the day of my party."

"Maybe you should have thought about that before you started World War Three with him last night."

Isabelle Thorndale looked like she was going to burst. Finally, she shook her head. "Then we'll just do the unveiling without him."

"What is this unveiling you keep talking about?" I asked.

Isabelle looked at me like I was stupid.

"It's the Knutsen I mentioned to you," Valerie explained.

"Oh, right, of course. The Knutsen is a . . . um . . ."

"It's a painting, you idiot," Isabelle said. "Once a year, out of the nobleness of my heart, I bring the Knutsen out of my house and display it up there on the stage for . . . the people."

She said the word "people" like it physically hurt.

"Cool. When's this happening?"

"Yes, Mother," Valerie said. "Seeing that Pimsey is probably gone, perhaps for good this time, when is this happening?"

"Now, Valerie. It's happening now. Go get Mr. Snoot."

"You trust Snoot to handle your painting?"

"Oh, God no. You and Clay can handle the painting. I need Snoot to open the room. Pimsey was the only one who ever opens that door."

"And do you know why? Because Pimsey is the only one who has a key to that room."

"Snoot's the head of security. Certainly he has a key."

"You only remember what you want to, don't you, Mother? You told Snoot you trusted him as much as you trusted a crap sandwich. Per your instructions, Pimsey was the only one with a key."

"Well, find some other way to get that door open."

"Do you have any suggestions?"

"Must I do everything around here?"

Valerie smiled. "Usually, yes."

"I don't know. I don't care. Have Clay kick the door down or something. Just get it open so I can show off my painting!"

"Of course. Anything else, Mother?"

"Yes, one thing. If you see that good-for-nothing butler of mine, give him a message—he's fired."

Valerie seemed to enjoy that.

With a wink at me, she wheeled around and walked over to a man in a cream-colored suit and light blue tie. He was about five ten with sandy blond hair, handsome with the windswept look of a lifelong surfer. Which was interesting, since Hopeless, Idaho, was not especially well known for its surfing.

"Is that Clay?" I asked Isabelle.

She squinted at me. "Yes, of course."

"And who exactly is Clay?"

She squinted even harder. "Clay is my son."

"Ah, I see. You have a son. Do you have any other children?"

Isabelle's eyes flashed. "*How* can a reporter for the *Hopeless News* not already have this information? We are the Thorndales!"

It was kind of fun to see the old lady get so riled up.

"Forgive me, ma'am. I just haven't been around for a very long time."

She let out a disgusted breath. "I suppose that's *some* explanation." She tilted her head toward Valerie and Clay. "Valerie's my oldest. Then Clay. Then . . ." She let the words hang a little. "Then there's my youngest. Kitty."

She didn't sound angry when she said it. But she did sound resigned. Maybe disappointed. And definitely hurt.

Valerie and Clay moved toward the house and waved at their mother to follow. She started after them, and I quickly fell in step beside her. I wasn't about to let Isabelle Thorndale out of my sight. The sooner I got my talking points from her and hustled out of there, the better.

"So, Mrs. Thorndale, Earl told me just to write whatever you wanted me to."

"Is there a question in there?"

"Did you happen to win the Westminster Dog Show in the last year?"

"What?"

"Maybe christen a new yacht?"

"Are you on drugs?"

"Just what kind of story would you like me to write? Maybe something on this painting people keep talking about?"

"The Knutsen."

"Exactly. Is it worth a lot of money?"

"Yes."

"How much?"

"I don't know."

"Why not?"

"For starters, you never know how much a piece of art is worth until it's sold at an auction."

"Then just spitball it for me."

"Did you just say 'spitball' in front of me?"

"Estimate it."

"I know what you meant."

"We talking five, ten thousand bucks?"

"You really are on drugs."

"Less than that?"

She stopped and turned, looking like she wanted to fight me. "No. *More* than that. What do you think I am, a country hick going on about some painting that's worth a few thousand dollars? The Knutsen is worth at least a million, and potentially far more."

"Really?"

"Yes, really. In fact, I just had it inspected and appraised yesterday by an expert from one of the premier auction houses in North America. He's going to tell me his official estimate today, at the unveiling."

"Oh! And you expect to be happy with his evaluation?"

"He *guaranteed* I would be happy."

I followed Mrs. Thorndale into the house through a side entrance. It opened into a foyer dominated by a beautiful wooden table holding a terra cotta statue of a cherub peeing into a basin of flowers. To our left was a large room filled with more statues and paintings and elaborate velvet couches and fancy French chairs. In front of us was a long corridor. And to our right was a closed wooden door and two people trying to open it.

Valerie was rattling the doorknob ineffectively, while Clay stood back as if sizing the door up.

"Are you going to stare it to death, Clay?" Isabelle asked.

Clay shot his mom a hateful look. But when he saw me, his expression changed. Embarrassment.

"Clay here is a lawyer," Isabelle said. "A very incompetent lawyer."

This woman truly was a delight.

A low, guttural sound came from Clay's throat. He stepped away from the door.

"Excuse me, Mother."

He took a deep breath, dragged his foot across the floor like you see bulls do in the cartoons, then ran at the door, his shoulder lowered. With a scream, he sent the door flying open.

I half expected to see smoke pouring out of his skull. But he just lay on the floor, holding his shoulder. I was impressed that he'd succeeded, but Isabelle buried her head in shame at his whimpering, and Valerie laughed.

"Get up, Clay," Isabelle scowled. "And for God's sake, conduct yourself with a little more . . . I don't know . . . class."

Clay rolled over and shot his mother another hateful look. Then he climbed to his feet and let out a shriek.

Valerie, Isabelle, and I all ran into the room.

I thought maybe something was wrong with the painting. But the Knutsen—which I could see immediately was an odd and not-at-all brilliant piece of art—was fine.

What was *not* fine was the man in the butler's suit lying on the floor in front of the Knutsen. Judging by his empty, lifeless stare and the large pool of blood around his head, he was not fine at all.

CHAPTER 9

Isabelle Thorndale screamed, Vivian Thorndale started to sob, and I immediately had two thoughts. First, I needed to stop finding dead people.

And second, at least we knew the butler didn't do it.

Clay turned to one side and threw up on the floor. That made me take several steps backwards. I was getting used to dead bodies.

But I would never get used to vomit.

The parade of horrified looks continued with none other than Mortimer Snoot. The head of security ran into the room and surveyed the scene. "What's Pimsey doing on the floor?"

This guy was a real crackerjack.

"And why is there ketchup all around him?"

That's when his eyes grew big. "That's not ketchup!"

I looked over at him. "You don't say?"

Mortimer Snoot screamed.

The smell of the vomit was starting to get to me, and now that a national security expert like Snoot was on the scene, I thought it might be a very good time to leave. But the circus wasn't quite done. Three more people ran into the room.

The first was the bartender, Mrs. Scratchett. The second was a woman wearing a white apron over a long gray dress. She looked kind of like the cook on *Downton Abbey*. The third was a small man wearing a three-piece suit, a bad toupee, and the kind of glasses one wears when trying very hard to look smart. All three of them spotted Pimsey at the same time. The *Downton Abbey* woman screamed while Scratchett and the man both covered their faces. It was beginning to feel like one of those clown cars—how many more people could we squeeze into this room?—and the scent of the vomit wasn't going anywhere. I needed to get out of there, and quick.

I skirted around the outside of the room and moved for the door. And that's when I ran smack-dab into one last person.

The sheriff of Hopeless, Idaho.

"Hope?" Alex said as my face collided with his chest. "I heard screams. What's going on?"

I looked up into his green eyes and knew that a picture was worth all the words I might think of. I stepped aside.

Judging by the expression on his face, Alex did not think we had stumbled upon a case of spilled ketchup.

He rushed to Pimsey's side, hit one knee, examined the body without touching it, and then looked around at the cast of characters.

"It would make my job a lot easier if one of you would just admit to killing him so I could go back out to the party and eat some food. No? No takers? Fine. Who found the body?"

He looked around once more at all the blank faces, and his gaze stopped on mine. "Hope, please tell me you didn't find the body."

"Okay, I won't."

"You've gotta be kidding me. Again?"

"Technically, it was Clay, Valerie, and Isabelle who found him first. I was just a spectator."

He closed his eyes and shook his head. I'm guessing he said a few curse words to himself as well. I have that effect on people.

He pointed past me. "I noticed the door's been busted in. Can someone explain that?"

Valerie spoke up. "We didn't have the key to the door. It was locked. And we needed to get in for the painting."

Alex rose to his feet, put his hands on his hips, and studied the painting. I did too. The world-famous, million-dollar Knutsen was nothing more than a cowboy riding a bucking bronco with an obnoxious splash of yellow behind it.

Granny once took me on a road trip to visit some distant relatives in Omaha. On the way, we passed through Cawker City, Kansas, so Granny could show me the world's largest ball of twine. It was pretty huge. I remember asking Granny how much she thought it was worth. She figured a few hundred bucks.

Still, that ball of twine was way more impressive than this rather simplistic painting.

By the look on his face, Alex agreed. He looked at Valerie. "And who broke the door?"

Valerie pointed to Clay, who was sitting on the floor with his head between his knees. "Clay busted it down!"

"Because you didn't have a key."

"That's right."

"Why didn't you just go get a key?"

"Because there's only one key. And the person who keeps that key wasn't around."

"And that person would be?"

"Mr. Pimsey, our butler. And as you can see, he's dead."

"Thank you, ma'am, for pointing that out." He looked at Clay again. "Is that puke?"

Clay nodded. His face looked a little green. "I'm sensitive to blood."

"So," Alex said, "allow me to sum up. The door was locked. Clay breaks the door down. Valerie, Isabelle, and Hope walk into the room. And they discover Pimsey, the butler, lying in a pool of his own blood."

Valerie nodded. "That's correct."

He surveyed the scene again, then turned to me. "Hope, did you touch anything?"

"You really think I would interfere with a murder investigation?"

"A thousand percent yes."

"Well, I didn't."

"Did anybody else touch the body?"

"No."

Alex took off his cowboy hat and ran a hand through his hair. "Okay, everybody, this is a crime scene. I need all of you to leave so I can seal off this room, get my equipment, and begin investigating. Wait—scratch that. Don't *leave* leave. You're all suspects. I need you to wait in the room across the hall until I get your statements."

"But I have a party to host," Isabelle said.

"Ma'am, there's a dead man in your house. That's a little more important than your party."

"Debatable. Can I at least have my painting so I can get it ready for the unveiling?"

"Mother!" Valerie said.

"What? It's not like Pimsey will mind."

"No, Mrs. Thorndale," Alex said, "you can't have the painting. Like I said, this is a crime scene, and I have to process it before we do anything. Now please, all of you, exit the scene and wait in the other room until I can get your statements."

Isabelle sniffed. "Well! I've never been treated so rudely in all my life."

Valerie had the decency to escort her mother out of the room. The others followed.

Alex beckoned me over. "I need a favor."

"Sorry, I can't teach you how to fire a gun right at the moment. I'm in the middle of a big story."

"I'm serious. Believe it or not, I wasn't expecting a dead body when I came to this party. I'm going out to the truck to grab what supplies I have and call Katie. She'll need to bring the other stuff from the office."

"And you need me to figure out who the killer is before you get back."

"I definitely do not need you to do that. I need you to babysit these people until I'm ready to take their statements."

"Babysit? Why, Alex Kramer, are you making me a deputy?"

"I knew this was a bad idea."

"Relax, I'll do it."

"Thanks. Oh, and Hope, I know I'm asking you to do me a favor . . . but . . . please, can you stay out of this one for me?"

"Little old me? I've already solved my quota of two small-town murders per year. You don't have to worry about me at all."

That, of course, was a lie. Granny had taught me long ago that asking forgiveness was often just as good as asking for permission—and was always a much more efficient way of getting things done. If solving a double murder wasn't enough to make a big-time newspaper crawl on its knees to hire me, then solving a third murder would seal the deal.

I was not a thieving fox sort of reporter.

I was a serious investigative reporter.

And as I walked out of the crime scene and scanned Isabelle Thorndale, her daughter Valerie, and the other possible suspects in this case, I remembered what Earl Denton had said—that this was the biggest story of the year. He just might be right.

No story was bigger than murder.

CHAPTER 10

The assembled suspects looked tired, bewildered, a little sad, and a lot rough. In other words, they looked like they *very much* wanted to speak with an annoying reporter like me. And despite what Alex had said, I was reminded of the famous quote that had become something of a life motto for my granny, and by extension, me.

Well-behaved women seldom make history.

Isabelle Thorndale stood in the center of the room in an argument with Valerie. It appeared Isabelle couldn't quite grasp why the presence of a murder victim in her house should interrupt her glorious party.

Clay had collapsed into a chair on the left side of the room. His suntanned face now looked mostly white, and his windswept hair was out of place. He was no longer a thirtysomething surfer, but a middle-aged drunk. The beer he pressed to his lips completed the look.

Mrs. Scratchett, part-time barmaid and full-time maid,

was arranging pillows on a couch, while the *Downton Abbey* cook sat on the end of the couch in stunned silence.

Mortimer Snoot was in a close conversation with the small, bespectacled man.

I took out my pad and pen and walked over to Isabelle Thorndale. I was sure everyone had the same question on their minds, so I might as well just come out and ask it.

"Mrs. Thorndale, who do you think killed Mr. Pimsey?"

She looked up abruptly like she wanted to strangle me. Which I was starting to learn was Isabelle Thorndale's normal face.

"I'm sure I have no idea. But if I knew that worthless Pimsey was going to go and get himself killed on the day of my party, I would have killed him myself!"

"So you admit to wanting to kill him?"

"Just about every day for the last thirty-nine years."

"And how long has he worked for you?"

"Thirty-nine years."

"You have a butler you called a buffoon earlier, who you regularly want to kill, and yet he's remained employed with you for over thirty years. How do you explain that?"

"Well, when you put it like that . . ." Isabelle turned to her daughter. "Valerie, why *didn't* I fire Pimsey years ago?"

"Because Pimsey is not a buffoon. He's a great butler, and he was willing to put up with your tyrannical nature. Besides, you *did* fire him. At least fifty times. You fired him three times on my tenth birthday alone."

"Oh, I do remember that. I kept on firing him, and the ungrateful snob never had the decency to leave."

Valerie rolled her eyes. "Or, to put it another way, Mother, he stayed despite your ridiculousness because he knew that without him, this family, this house, and you would fall apart."

"Nonsense."

Time for another question. "I understand, Mrs. Thorndale, that you and Mr. Pimsey got into an argument last night. What was it about?"

"I don't think that's any of your business," Isabelle said.

"Fine, but let *me* paint you a picture," I said. "You have a man you've shown disdain for in the past. Last night, you get into a big argument with him. And today, he's found murdered."

"What's your point?"

"I think you know my point. You may not have to tell *me* what your argument with Pimsey was about, but you will have to tell Sheriff Kramer. Why not do a dress rehearsal with me?"

Isabelle looked as though my words had put a bad taste in her mouth. She sucked a breath through her nose, turned her head to the side for a beat, then came back to me. "When will Sheriff Kramer be done in there? I need to get my painting."

"You really care that much about your painting right now? I mean, a man you've known for a very long time is dead."

"That's right, Miss Walker. He's dead. Meaning there's nothing I can do about it. But my painting is very much alive, and it's worth a lot of money. I'd like to keep it that way."

Talking to this woman was like talking to a brick wall. A very pompous and angry brick wall.

I turned my sights on Mortimer Snoot, international man of mystery. "Mr. Snoot," I said, interrupting his conversation with the bespectacled man.

"You!" he sneered.

"Yes, me. At least I think it's me. No . . . yes, I'm certain of it. Mr. Snoot, I figured since you solved the case of the kicked giblets, you might have an idea who killed Mr. Pimsey."

His mouth opened, then closed again. Clearly he didn't know what to say.

"You're not telling me that the Thorndales' head of security not only allowed a murder to occur on his watch, but he has no idea who did it?"

"I—I have my suspicions," he stammered.

"And would you care to share them?"

"No, I would not. Especially not with you."

"Too bad. That was your chance to exonerate yourself."

"What are you talking about?"

"Oh, come off it, Mr. Snoot," I said rather loudly. "Everybody knows about the time you promised to kill Pimsey at the foot of that ridiculous painting."

Everyone in the room turned to us for a long and awkward moment before returning to their own conversations.

"It's not a ridiculous painting," chirped the small man.

"And you are?"

He looked at me and my outfit like he thought I might be contagious. "My name is Anton Sokolov. I work for

Billingham's Auction House. That's in San Francisco. The bigger question is, who are *you*?"

"My name is Hope Walker. I work for the *Hopeless News*. That's not in San Francisco. I'm here because Mrs. Thorndale wants us to cover her party. And I have to say, so far, it hasn't disappointed."

"Do you know when we'll be allowed to go back in there and examine the painting?"

"You and Mrs. Thorndale sure are nervous about that painting."

"That's because it's very *valuable*. I want to make sure nothing happens to it while that brute of a sheriff is alone with it."

"I really don't understand that painting. You say it's worth a lot of money, and everybody keeps telling me it's famous, and I can't figure out why."

Mr. Sokolov sneered at me. "It's a Knutsen."

"I'm getting a little tired of people saying that like it's supposed to mean something to me. I looked at that painting. It's just a guy on a horse."

A little noise came from the back of Sokolov's throat. He leaned in toward me. "It is *not* 'just a guy on a horse,'" he said through gritted teeth.

"Then I must not get it."

"Obviously. And as much as it pains me, I will do my level best to *help* you get it. But I'm only going through this once. Irek Knutsen was a pioneering western artist. He was famous for his abstract sculptures, his essays on cowboys, and his black-and-white photographs of cats trying to flush the toilet."

"You're not serious."

"I am. Knutsen was truly revolutionary. He was doing cats flushing the toilet in the 1950s, long before every idiot with an iPhone was vlogging their felines in real time. Now, there had always been rumors that he *painted* as well, but it wasn't until he died that this was proven, when his estate released three of his paintings. All three were sold privately to a museum in London. The estate said there was a handful more, and they would be released to public auction over a period of a few years. There are now precisely six in circulation. The original three, which are still at the London museum. One that's owned by an oilman in Dallas. One by a furniture magnate in North Carolina. And one owned by none other than Isabelle Thorndale."

"But . . . it's a guy on a horse."

Mr. Sokolov's face reddened. "It's not a guy on a horse! It's a *famous* painting by an *important* artist that at auction would probably fetch somewhere in the neighborhood of ten million dollars!" Sokolov had worked himself up into quite a lather, and everyone in the room looked in our direction yet again.

"Ten million dollars!" Isabelle shrieked. "Are you talking about my Knutsen? Are you saying it's worth ten million dollars?"

Mr. Sokolov was suddenly on the spot. He tugged at his collar nervously. "I had wanted to save the good news for today's unveiling, but yes, Mrs. Thorndale, based on the condition of the painting and the contacts I've made, ten million dollars is a conservative estimate."

"Conservative?"

"I believe under the right conditions, a motivated collector would be willing to pay more."

Isabelle's eyes were suddenly wet, and the old bag couldn't help it—her mouth turned upward into a smile.

Expensive painting, one. Dead butler, zero.

"Seriously, though—am I missing something?" I said. "Does this painting fold out into a five-thousand-square-foot Manhattan penthouse?"

"Yes," Sokolov said. "You are missing something. Collectors and museums decided long ago that paintings from Irek Knutsen were important. There is a very small supply of such paintings. Therefore, each and every Knutsen painting is virtually priceless."

Isabelle was clearly determined to talk to Mr. Sokolov about her precious priceless painting, so I left them alone and walked over to the women at the far end of the room. Mrs. Scratchett was fiddling with the flowers on the table behind the couch. *Downton Abbey* was up now, pacing in front of the couch.

"I didn't catch your name," I said.

"Hannah Schneider. I'm the cook."

I was right about the cook part.

"Had you known Mr. Pimsey long?"

She ran her hands down her apron like she was drying them off, then nodded her head. "Fifteen years. As long as I've worked here."

Mrs. Scratchett put the flowers down. "It's been over twenty years for me. I can hardly believe it."

"And would either of you . . ."

"Have any idea who killed him?" Mrs. Schneider said. "I've been racking my brain about that."

"And what have you come up with?"

"Nothing so far. But I do have a question. What was Pimsey doing in that room?"

"What do you mean?"

"That's a good question," Mrs. Scratchett said. "Today's the party, and Pimsey's the one who takes that stupid painting out for the unveiling—but not until today, and not until the old bag tells him to."

"Maybe he was just checking on it?" I offered.

"I don't know," Mrs. Schneider said. "Pimsey was a man of routine. He'd only check on the painting if he thought there was a specific reason. Mrs. Scratchett, to your knowledge, how often does anyone go into that room?"

"Once a month, Pimsey goes in there with me so I can clean and dust. But he always watches me like a hawk because he knows Mrs. Thorndale would freak if anything happened to that stupid painting. Other than that? I think he lets Mrs. Thorndale in to look at it every once in a while. But mostly, it just sits there all alone, waiting for its big day."

"The unveiling," I said.

"Exactly."

"Did anybody have a particular beef with Pimsey?" I asked.

"You mean, did anybody have motive?" Mrs. Schneider said.

"Yes."

"He and Mrs. Thorndale never seemed to get along," Mrs. Scratchett said.

"But she would never kill him," Mrs. Schneider said.

"Or at least, she would never kill him so close to her precious painting."

Mrs. Scratchett shrugged. "I don't know. Maybe . . ."

"Maybe what?" I said.

"Well, Mrs. Thorndale and Pimsey got into it last night. I could hear the shouting from the living room. I saw Pimsey when he came down from her quarters. He was fuming."

"So what?" Mrs. Schneider asked.

"What if he was so angry that he decided to go down there and do something to her precious painting? Or worse, steal it?"

Mrs. Schneider's eyes grew wide. "And what if Mrs. Thorndale followed him, saw what he was about to do, and smacked him!"

Scratchett snapped her fingers. "She doesn't mean to kill him, but she does. And then she's not strong enough to move him."

Schneider bounced up on her tiptoes. "So she grabs his key, locks the room back up, and waits until today for his body to be discovered."

"That actually makes a lot of sense," I said. "The two of you should be detectives. Scratchett and Schneider."

Mrs. Schneider smiled, but Mrs. Scratchett held out her hands. "And leave the glamour of cooking and cleaning for spoiled rich people? How could we possibly give up the good life?"

CHAPTER 11

Through the doorway, I saw Dr. Bridges come into the house and enter the room where Pimsey's body lay. I wondered how long it was going to be before my babysitting gig was over. Isabelle Thorndale and her merry band wouldn't want to stay here much longer.

But as long as I was here, there was one person I had yet to visit with. He was still slouched into a chair, nursing his beer.

"It's Clay, right?"

He covered his eyes. "I'm sorry you had to see that back there."

"The getting sick? Don't worry about it. Seeing a dead body, that's enough to make anybody get sick."

"But I'm the only one who did." He looked away. "I have never done well around blood."

"I hear Pimsey's been the butler here for a long time."

"Ever since Mother and Dad built this place, since before I was born."

"That's a long time to be someone's butler. Especially when it seems like they hated each other."

His eyebrows narrowed, and he set down his beer. "Who told you that?"

"It's the general vibe I get."

Clay chuckled. "Listen, my mother is not an easy woman, but part of her deal is, she likes people she can joust with. Pimsey was tough. He could hold his own. Sure, they went back and forth a lot, but I think secretly, they liked each other."

"You mean, they *like* liked each other?"

"No. I mean they had a . . . begrudging admiration for each other. Like family. Yep, no doubt about it." Clay picked up his now-empty beer bottle and tipped it to no one in particular. "Pimsey, he was family."

"So, who would do this to him?"

"Not family." He stood up and extended his hand. "I'm afraid I didn't make a good first impression with the whole vomit-on-the-crime-scene thing. How about we start over and I properly introduce myself. Clay Thorndale."

"Hope Walker."

"I know."

"You heard about me solving those two murders?"

"Actually, I remember you."

"What do you mean, you remember me?"

"As a kid. I was only a few years older than you."

"But you didn't go to school here. If I remember correctly, you guys all went to some boarding school."

"In Spokane. Valerie and Kitty went to the Northridge

School for Girls, and I went to the Holland School for Boys."

"They sound like snooty schools."

"They were," he agreed.

"Then how do you remember me?"

"I saw you at the pool one summer. I thought you were cute."

"Ah. So you were a creeper."

"I was only three years older than you. I'm not sure that qualifies as a creeper."

"Wait a second. Were you that boy who would do all those crazy flips off the high dive?"

Clay smiled proudly, and I do believe his chest puffed out a little. "So you remember me too."

I hesitated. It was fun to see men puffed up just before the body blow. "Nah, there was always some idiot boy showing off for the girls by doing flips off the diving board."

The smile was erased from his face, and his shoulders slumped. "That hurts."

"I'm sure you'll get over it. So, no idea who might have done this to Pimsey?"

"Only one idea. The way I figure it, somebody broke in to steal the painting, and Pimsey caught him . . . and lost his life over it."

"But if that's true, why is the painting still here?"

Clay shrugged. "That's a good point. I guess the sheriff will have to figure it out."

Not if I figure it out first.

Valerie stepped over to join us. "Any idea how long this is going to take?"

"I'll check in with the sheriff in a minute. How are you dealing with all of this?"

Valerie looked choked up. "Not very well. Whatever my mother may say, Pimsey was a dear man. He didn't deserve this."

"Your brother says Pimsey was family."

Valerie nodded soberly. "Yes, family. That's exactly it."

A terrible sound came from the foyer. I turned to see a young woman, her black hair pulled back into a ponytail, doubled over, sobbing as she looked in at the crime scene. Juan was with her, and he grabbed her and turned her away. Dark sunglasses covered her eyes, but the rest of her face was pale as milk, and she continued to sob hysterically. Juan ushered her into our room, and Clay went to her and gave her a big hug.

Juan looked around as if to get some answers. I beckoned him over with my head.

"Pimsey's dead?" he said in disbelief.

"We found him about twenty minutes ago."

"Any idea what happened?"

"None. Did you know him well?"

"Not really. I spend most of my time outside. He hired me, and I had occasional interactions with him, but not much."

"And how'd you get along?"

"Fine. When he had something for me to do, I did it. That was pretty much the extent of our relationship."

Clay was still holding the girl, and Valerie had joined them and was rubbing the girl's back. Both were trying to console her. Clearly, this must be the younger sister.

"That's Kitty?" I asked Juan.

"Yes. She just drove up to the parking area, and one of the guests who was leaving said that the sheriff was needed in the house for some type of emergency, so I walked up with her to see what was going on."

"Any idea who might have done something like this?"

Juan shook his head. "Heavens, no."

I walked over to Kitty. Clay and Valeria had released her, and she was now just standing there in stunned silence.

"I'm so sorry," I said. "You and Pimsey must have been close."

"Who are you?" Her expression was not dissimilar from the one permanently on the face of her mother.

"My name is Hope Walker. The sheriff asked me to stay with you all until he and the doctor are finished. Then the sheriff will come in here to get statements from everyone."

"Statements?"

"It's nothing to be worried about. In order to get to the bottom of what happened, he just needs to talk to everyone."

Isabelle suddenly joined us. Why she hadn't come over to comfort her obviously distraught daughter earlier, I didn't know. Perhaps she deliberately waited until Kitty had composed herself in order to avoid having to fake an unfamiliar emotion such as compassion.

"Kitty," she said. "Juan said you just got here."

Kitty looked at her mom, then at me. Her eyes were suddenly fidgety. "Yes. I was in Boise."

"So, Kitty," I said, "I take it you and Pimsey were close?"

"He was always nice to me. Always."

"I'm sorry to ask, but can you think of anybody who might have wanted to hurt him?"

Her eyes narrowed, and she glared at her mother. "Take a wild guess."

Then Kitty Thorndale walked away, sat down on a chair, and stared out the window.

I POKED my head into the crime scene to see what was taking so long. Dr. Bridges was gloved up, on his knees, doing an inspection of the old butler. Alex hovered impatiently above.

Finally, Dr. Bridges looked up from the body. "Yep, definitely dead."

"The lack of a pulse sort of gave that away, Doc. Cause of death?"

"I'm afraid it's Sheriff Kline all over again."

"Blunt force trauma to the head."

Dr. Bridges pointed to the side of Pimsey's head. "A nasty blow right here."

"Murder weapon?"

Bridges looked around the room and shrugged. "Your guess is as good as mine. But it was something heavy. Dense."

"Time of death?"

"When was the last time anybody saw Mr. Pimsey?"

"Seriously, Doc? That's the best you can do?"

"I'm not a forensic scientist, Alex. I'll get him back to

the lab and take a temperature of his liver, and then I'll have a better idea."

"But you'll collect forensic evidence first?"

"Fibers, hairs, the whole nine yards."

"I thought you said you weren't a forensic scientist."

"Hey, an old dog can learn some new tricks. I'll collect whatever I find and send it off to your friends at the state police lab."

"Thanks, Doc."

Dr. Bridges noticed me and gave me a friendly wave. Alex turned my way and shook his head. "Hope, why do you keep finding dead bodies?"

"Sheriff, I believe the better question is, when are you going to deputize me so I can solve all your crimes for you?"

"How about never? Seriously, Hope. This time I just want you to let me do my job. I appreciate you babysitting my suspects. Thank you. But now, I'm going to start investigating a murder, and you're going to go home and *not* find any more dead bodies."

"I respectfully decline. As a reporter for the *Hopeless News*, I have a right to be here and cover this story."

"No, you don't. I'm asking you to leave."

"You're kicking me out?"

"Yes. As hard as this is to believe, I, Sheriff Kramer, a member of law enforcement, am asking you, a reporter, to leave the scene of a crime."

He gave me that jerky hand gesture people give you when they're politely asking you to leave.

"Keep it up, Sheriff Kramer, and I'll tell Katie not to get you flowers for the next Boss Appreciation Day."

He folded his arms and glared at me. But I wasn't about to budge. Alex Kramer would soon learn that in any contest of wills, I was the immovable rock.

Finally he shook his head in frustration, marched over, grabbed me by the arm, and hustled me away. Out of the crime scene room, past the cherub peeing into the terra cotta basin, and to the house's side door.

It was there that I shook his arm off. "Fine. I'll just exercise my constitutional right to solve the case without looking at the crime scene. Goodbye, Dr. Bridges," I called out. "Goodbye, dead butler guy." I gave Alex my best glare. "And goodbye to you, Sheriff."

I stalked away from the house in my bright yellow *Hopeless News* vest. I was tired, sweaty, I smelled quite a bit, and I looked like a night-light. Or a lampshade. Depends on who you asked. I had a hundred-year-old farmhouse that I was supposed to paint. I had a Big Story about a rich old lady's party that I was supposed to write. And yet, all I could think about was the *real* Big Story. The one that was lying dead in front of a ten-million-dollar painting that Katie's children could probably have made if given the right kind of markers.

I stopped and surveyed the Thorndales' mighty green lawn. It seemed the party was going on just fine without the Thorndales themselves. Either everyone was oblivious to the corpse inside the house, or they simply didn't care. I thought about diving into the crowd, asking questions about Pimsey, and trying to figure out an angle to this story.

But then I realized, I really did stink quite a bit.

What I needed at that very moment wasn't a story.

I needed a shower.

I passed through the main gate, walked to my car, and drove off. I went down Frampton Road, through town, and back to the Library. And just as I parked my car and prepared to get out, I noticed that something had fallen on the floor of my car. It was a note.

So much had happened that day, I'd almost forgotten about this strange little note. I picked it up and read it again.

I didn't mean to do it.

And I realized this might not *just* be some strange little note.

I might be holding a confession.

CHAPTER 12

I woke up the next morning with a spring in my step. It was Sunday, and I had in my possession what I was pretty sure was a key piece of evidence in Hopeless, Idaho's latest murder. And if I could crack this story in record time? That ought to be enough to open the doors to a big-city investigative reporter job.

Not to mention, it would royally get under the skin of our town's newest sheriff.

I drove down to A Hopeless Cup, purveyor of my favorite cup of coffee since I'd come back to town. But today, I wasn't there for the coffee. Well, not *only* the coffee. I was there because of what I'd learned the week before, when I cracked my first murder case in Hopeless.

A Hopeless Cup had a camera pointed down Main Street in the general direction of the Library. They used it to create one of those cool time-lapse videos that they played on a TV screen outside their store. It was part of their effort to provide the best view in Hopeless.

Whoever slipped this note under the Library's door would be on that camera.

Thank goodness criminals were dumb.

I went in hoping to find Nick, Generation Z's most annoying barista. But all I found was Madeline, a twenty-year-old girl with tattoos covering one side of her body and piercings covering the other.

"I need a favor," I said.

"What?" she asked in the world's least pleasant voice.

"Nick already showed me, so it's not a big deal. I was just wondering if I could go in the back and look at the footage from your video cameras."

"Are you insane?"

"Call Nick. He won't mind."

"I don't know anybody who makes phone calls anymore."

"Fine. Text him."

She rolled her eyes. "People don't text anymore."

"They don't?"

"Nick said you were difficult. No, they Snap."

"Fine. Could you Snap him for me?"

"It's no use. We don't have the cameras anymore."

"Yes, you do. I saw them out front."

"I mean they're not taping anymore. After those murders that old lady solved."

"That was me. I'm the old lady."

"Yeah, whatever. After that, the ACLU threatened to sue us because we were violating people's privacy, so we stopped recording video."

Okay, then—it seemed my investigation wasn't going to be as easy as I thought. And why would it?

I needed to start at the beginning. Which meant, back to square one. Getting a cup of coffee. The one thing Madeline was good for.

And with coffee in hand, it was on to square two. Starting my investigation where all great investigations began.

Breakfast.

I found Granny holding court at her usual table at Buck's Diner. As it was Sunday, many people had either come from church or were getting ready to go to a later service, and were in their Sunday best. Granny was not most people. As usual, she was wearing her bright blue Boise State Football sweatshirt. Bess sat on her left in a simple brown dress, and Zeke Roberson was on her right in an old gray blazer. Flo from the hair salon completed their group. Buck hovered over all of them, dish towel slung over his shoulder, filling up coffee and grabbing used plates.

When Granny saw me, she waved. "Big eater's in the diner, Buck."

Buck looked my way and smiled. "Another Hangover Special?"

"For the record, I am not hung over. Nevertheless, I would very much like the Hangover Special."

I grabbed a sausage link off Granny's plate before she could swat my hand away, then sat between Zeke and Flo.

"Don't you normally fraternize with those tooty-fruity cappuccino folks in Tourist Town for breakfast?" Granny asked.

I was glad I'd drained my A Hopeless Cup coffee and ditched my paper cup before arriving. "What?" I said, trying my best to sound offended. “And miss eating breakfast with the only family I’ve ever known?”

Granny rolled her eyes. “Okay, out with it. What happened? You’re pregnant, aren’t you?”

“Nope.”

“But you need something from us. Okay, folks, pony up. Hope needs a one-way ticket out of the country for some dastardly crime she committed.”

“Granny, I do believe that’s the first time “dastardly’ has been used in a sentence this century.”

“Bess, was that a crack about me being old?”

Bess nodded.

“I’ve got it,” Granny said. She slapped the table with her hand. “You plan on accusing our mayor of double murder someplace super embarrassing, like, say, a funeral.”

“You’re really not going to let me forget that, are you?”

“I’ve never seen Wilma so mad in all my life.” Granny cackled. “It was fantastic.”

Buck slid a plate of eggs, bacon, sausage, and pancakes in front of me, then poured me a mug of hot black coffee. You can never have too much coffee. But first, I crammed a slice of bacon into my mouth.

“Actually, I was kind of wondering if you all had heard.”

“About the dead butler? I knew it. We need to get Hope out on the next flight to Mexico.”

“I find it disturbing that you keep thinking I’m committing murders around town.”

Granny shrugged. “Now you know how Wilma feels.”

“For the record, I did not commit this crime. Neither

did Mayor Jenkins. Well, as far as I know. After all, this is just one murder, and as we all know, her MO is double murders. Anyway, I need the geniuses at Buck's Diner to help me figure out what happened."

We decided that in keeping with the tradition started with Ed Kline's murder, the fallen-down ketchup bottle would represent the murder victim. But when deciding what should represent Isabelle Thorndale, the conversation quickly broke down. Granny thought she should be a black cup of coffee—to represent her "coal-black soul." Zeke thought she should be a bottle of vinegar because of the way she made you feel every time you talked to her. And Flo thought she should be a steaming pile of poo. Turns out Isabelle had come to Flo's shop years earlier for a haircut and was so disgusted that she proclaimed to everyone who would listen that a blind dog could cut hair better than Flo.

When Buck informed Flo that he hadn't kept a steaming pile of poo at the diner for years, everybody except Flo laughed.

It was Buck who decided that vinegar was the best choice. So we assembled vinegar, coffee, hot sauce, salt, pepper, a Splenda packet, a jar of maple syrup, and a packet of cream and commenced the Official Buck's Diner Inquiry into the Death of Mr. Pimsey, the Butler.

"So you found Pimsey on the floor right in front of that god-awful painting?" Granny asked.

"Yes," I said. "The painting was still there."

"Maybe Pimsey *thought* about stealing the painting, then thumped himself on the head when he realized how ugly it was," Buck said.

"Hmm. Suicide by blunt-force trauma. That would be a new one."

"Pimsey's the butler of that house," Zeke said. "It's his job to make sure everything is as it should be. Maybe he walked in as someone was trying to steal the painting. There's a struggle, the thief whacks him with something, and then the thief gets spooked and instead of stealing the painting, he just gets out of there."

"So in that case, the killer could be anyone. Just some anonymous thief?"

"Do we have anything to represent an anonymous thief?" Flo asked.

Granny snapped her fingers at Buck. "You got any meatloaf left over from yesterday?"

"Sure. Why?"

"Your meatloaf's tasteless, Buck. Have no idea what it's supposed to taste like. I figure we could use a plate of that for our anonymous killer."

Buck frowned. "That's low, Granny, even for you."

"I used half a bottle of ketchup on that meat slab. Get offended if you want—I'm just callin' it like I taste it."

"Okay," I continued. "But let's say it *wasn't* an anonymous thief. If it was someone in the house, who do you think it could have been?"

"What's the name of that creepy security guard you kicked in the 'nads back in high school?" Granny asked.

"Snoot. Mortimer Snoot."

"For real?"

I shrugged.

"I bet his poor mother gave him that name because she

knew he'd grow up to be a murderer. My money's on him."

"Kitty Thorndale used to come in the salon when she was younger," Flo said. "She'd talk, and I would listen. If I remember right, the maid, Mrs. Scratchett, didn't like Pimsey very much."

"Not surprising," Zeke said. "Back when I ran the general store, Mr. Pimsey came in once a month. Stern. Grouchy. Kind of miserable, if you ask me."

"Meaning?"

"I only had to deal with him once a month. Think about the people who lived and worked with him every day. I bet *any* of them could have killed him. Even old Mrs. Thorndale herself."

"You really think Isabelle could have killed him?"

They all looked at me blankly.

"Okay," I said, "I get it. I met her. She's horrible. Okay, she's *really* horrible. But she's also an old lady."

"Don't let the old lady thing fool you," Granny said. "I'm an old lady, but I could still kick your scrawny self all over the yard."

"Wait. Yesterday I had a big butt, and now I'm scrawny?"

"Yeah, you're scrawny *except* for your big butt. Point is, Isabelle Thorndale might be nasty, but she's also tough. After nuclear war, only two things will survive—cockroaches and Mrs. Thorndale."

"So, you really think this old bottle of vinegar could bash a man's head in?" I asked.

"Yes," Granny said. "I do."

We kept discussing the case, but we didn't get very far.

Finally, Granny checked the time. "Okay, folks. By my watch, there's only one hundred and forty-six hours left until thirteen years."

"Thirteen years of what?" Zeke asked.

"I told Hope that she would not finish painting my house in thirteen years. And in one hundred and forty-six hours, I will have been proven right."

I stood up, shoved a slice of bacon into my mouth, and threw my pancake at Granny like a Frisbee.

"What's this for?"

"This time," I said, "*you're* the big fat pancake. Because scrawny me and my big butt have a house to paint."

CHAPTER 13

Of course, there was one little problem. As much as I hated Granny giving me crap about not painting the house, I didn't actually *want* to paint the house. And now that a big story had popped up in the form of a dead butler, I had even less motivation to finish the job.

I needed help.

I needed my best friend.

I found Katie in her kitchen, cleaning up after what appeared to be the Sunday brunch from hell. She was standing on a chair, scraping scrambled eggs off the wall. The floor was littered with Cheerios. A stream of orange juice ran diagonally from one end of the kitchen to the other.

I was about to say something, but she cut me off with an aggressive finger. "Not a word. Not one word."

"So you get to make fun of my butt while I paint, but I can't comment on your interior decorating skills?"

She threw me a wet rag. "Now you're helping."

"Is that Aunt Hope?" I heard Dominic yell from the corner.

"So this is officially a thing now?" I said to Katie. "I'm *Aunt* Hope?"

"Not in a good way," Katie said. "We're talking about the aunt who doesn't have a job and smells funny. That kind of aunt."

"I take it young Skywalker had something to do with *eggs over ceiling*?"

Katie made a face. "It started out harmless enough—your typical bacon sword fight between him and Lucy. But then he rigged up some sort of . . ." She closed her eyes and shook her head. " . . . catapult system. Eggs were flying all over the place. That's when Celia got into the act. Cheerios filled the air like confetti in a ticker tape parade. I gave Chris the 'Aren't you going to do something' look, so of course he said he really had to go to the bathroom. And as I was yelling at Chris, Dominic got the bright idea to weaponize the orange juice. That's when things went nuclear."

"Only *then* it went nuclear? What do you call the flying eggs and Cheerios?"

"I call that eating breakfast with children."

"Where's Chris now?"

"I made him take Lucy and Celia to the park. He hates taking kids to the park. I think I'll make him stay there until Tuesday."

I nodded. "And Dominic?"

"I told him if he can stand in the corner until he's eighteen, I'll go ahead and pay for his college."

"You think you'll be able to afford college?"

She covered her mouth and whispered. "Oh, hell no, but he's only five. He doesn't know that."

"Can I get out of the corner now?" Dominic yelled from the other room.

"Do you promise to never, ever throw food at the table ever again?"

"Yes!"

"Are you lying?"

"Probably."

Katie looked at me. "He's ethically challenged, yet compulsively honest. I kind of admire that."

"Don't you think this would go faster if we made him help us?" I suggested.

"Oh, you with your zero kids are now the parenting expert?"

"No, but this is a lot of orange juice. I was thinking I could roll Dominic across the floor . . . use him like a squeegee."

"*Now* you're thinking like a parent. I like it. Dominic, you know your dad's favorite sweatshirt?"

"The really ugly green one?"

"Yep! Go upstairs, put it on, and run back here."

Dominic's feet pounded up the stairs.

"It's a Sunday, and you're helping me clean up Brunch-mageddon," Katie said. "What's up?"

"We haven't had a chance to talk about the big news yet."

"The news about a third dead body in less than two weeks?"

"What are the odds, right?"

"Not very good in a town our size."

"Speaking of a town our size, any ideas who might have done it?"

"Hope, look at me. I'm wearing a Buck's Diner T-shirt I won in a raffle, it's stained, and I'm scraping scrambled eggs off the wall. You really think I have any insight into the lives of the rich and famous?"

"Come on, Katie, you've lived here your whole life. You must know something about these people."

She stopped and leveled a serious stare my way. "Only one thing." She broke into a smile. "At least we know the butler didn't do it."

"Sorry, I've already used that joke. Nobody laughed. Hey, you know the best part? And by best, I mean worst?"

"The butler was going to take you on your first real date in twelve years, and now you're back to square one?"

"My life is not that pathetic."

"You're on your knees cleaning up orange juice from somebody else's kid on a Sunday."

"Okay, I'm a little pathetic."

"Oh, don't worry. I'm the queen of pathetic. This morning, I washed every single sheet in our house because everybody peed in their beds last night. Even me! And I'm pretty sure my yeast infection could be weaponized for biological warfare. So trust me, you're just marginally pathetic by comparison. Like one of my henchmen. Just tell me the best-worst part."

"The best-worst part is, I was there when the body was found. You know how some women are guy magnets? Apparently, I'm a dead body magnet."

"Shut the front door! So, what happened?"

"Somebody caved the poor guy's head in. Other than

that, I have no idea. Sheriff Crinkly Clothes threw me out before I could get my story on. Why'd you get him such nerdy sheriff's clothes?"

Katie winced. "Yeah, the new uniform really doesn't flatter him, does it? Also, I just remembered I'm not supposed to talk to you about the investigation. Not to anyone, really, but the sheriff specifically mentioned you."

"That's ridiculous. This is a big case with an even bigger story. Of *course* you're going to talk to me about it."

"Sorry, Hope. Sheriff Kramer was clear. Not only am I not to talk to you about *this* investigation, but I'm not to talk to you about any investigation in the history of the world. Amelia Earhart. Bigfoot. Even the moon landing. He said we can't talk about it."

"There's no way that moon landing was real."

"I know! *Had* to be done in a studio, right?"

"Right. And if you saw Bigfoot . . ."

"You mean *if I saw Bigfoot again*? I will show you my grainy black-and-white photos."

"See? He can't keep us from talking," I said. "It's ridiculous. Almost as ridiculous as those starched sheriff's clothes."

"I already admitted it's not the best look on him."

"You think? You made him look like Ed Kline Junior."

"So, Alex Kramer doesn't want you anywhere near his investigation and he wears dorky clothes. It seems his only redeeming traits are his wide shoulders, sparkly green eyes, chiseled jaw, long legs, and perfect butt."

I snapped my towel at Katie. "Katie Rodgers, you're a married woman."

"With a thirty-year mortgage and what feels like a

five-year-old bladder infection. So by God, if I see a man with a perfect butt, I'm going to say it loud and say it proud, no matter how many workplace rules it violates."

"But maybe you could find him a new uniform," I suggested.

"And maybe you could find some way of investigating a murder that doesn't involve pumping me for information."

"Oh, I'm going after this story, that's for sure. But I've got two problems. The first is Sheriff Kramer. The second is, I've got to finish painting Granny's house by noon on Saturday."

"Or else?"

"Or she'll be proven right."

"Well, we wouldn't want that."

"As a matter of fact, Katie, no, we would not. She's the absolute worst at gloating, and I'll never hear the end of it for the rest of my life. 'Hope never finishes what she starts.'"

"So, why are you here instead of at Granny's?"

I said nothing. I just looked up at Katie and smiled.

"Oh, no. No way."

"It's the only chance I've got, Katie. I need help."

"There is no way I am getting my fat keister up on a ladder to help you paint that house."

"I thought *I* was the one with the big butt."

"You have a big butt only in an ironical sort of way. Like, hey, my gorgeous skinny best friend doesn't have a perfect butt anymore. Yay! But me? My bottom was plenty plump to begin with, and now, after three kids?

Have you seen Celia's head? Nothing good can come from pushing that through your you-know-what."

"Nothing good except a unique and eternal soul."

She rolled her eyes, then made the sign of the cross. "Except for that."

"You gonna help me or not?"

"Definitely not."

"That's what our friendship means to you?"

"I'll make you a deal." Katie smiled. "I'll help you in twelve years."

"So, we're really not done with those jokes yet?"

Katie finally got down from the chair. "Honey, we're just getting started."

Dominic ran into the kitchen wearing an old green sweatshirt that hung down to his knees. "What do I do now, Mama?"

Katie pulled the hoodie over his head and tied it in front. Then she crouched down and put her arm around him. "Remember last summer when we had the slip-and-slide in the backyard?"

"Yes."

"Well, consider the kitchen floor your slip-and-slide. And the orange juice? It's your water."

"For real?"

Katie grabbed her purse. "For real. And Dominic, when all the orange juice is off the floor, walk down the block to the park and tell Dad that Hope and I went out for a bit."

"Sure thing, Mama."

"Oh, and one more thing. Be sure to give your dad a big hug."

I followed Katie out the door. "Does this mean you're going to help me paint?" I asked.

"This means I'm going to drink beer out of Granny's fridge, hand you paint when you need it, and generally support you. I will *not* be doing any painting. But . . . I promise not to make fun of you. Much."

I was about to thank Katie when her phone buzzed. She pulled it out of her purse, read a text message, then looked up at me. "I really shouldn't tell you this."

"Tell me what?"

"Seems that Sheriff Kramer's wrapping up at the Thorndales' and heading home for a nap. He reminded me not to tell you anything."

I smiled despite myself.

"I take it you're not smiling because you're excited to go paint your granny's house?" Katie said.

"You know me better than that."

"Unfortunately, I do. Just promise not to get me in trouble."

"I think you also know me better than that."

Katie sighed.

"You going to join your family down at the park?"

"I'm going to go to bed and take a nap as well. Apparently, it's company policy."

"What constitutes 'long' for a busy mom of three?"

"Fifteen minutes, if I'm lucky." She patted me on the back. "Go get 'em, Hope."

CHAPTER 14

I parked far down the block so Sheriff Kramer wouldn't be able to spot my car. I only had to wait a few minutes before he came out of the Thorndales' mansion carrying a large briefcase. He put the case in his pickup truck, eased out of the driveway, and drove down the street. Had he really been there all night? If so, hopefully he'd be going down for a very long siesta.

Which meant I had the Thorndales all to myself. I parked closer to the house, slipped through the front gate, and walked to the side entrance. Yellow police tape was set up, but I was taking that as more of a suggestion than anything else.

I knocked and waited only a moment before the door opened. It was Valerie.

"Hope? What are you doing here?"

"I'll be honest with you, Valerie. I *could* tell you I'm here because Earl Denton is making me finish this story on your mother and her party. And of course that's true.

But the reality is, there was a murder here —and that's a pretty big story."

"And you want to cover it."

"I'm an investigative reporter. It's sort of my duty to cover it."

She hesitated, then opened the door farther. "Fine. Sheriff Kramer just left. Mother is checking on her Knutsen. Come on in."

I stepped inside, politely waved to the cherub peeing in the basin, then turned to the broken door. There was powder all over the knob and lock plate, the telltale signs of where Sheriff Kramer had been dusting for prints.

Valerie led me right through the doorway to the crime scene. The dead butler was gone. By now Dr. Bridges would have taken him. And the blood had all been cleaned up. I half expected the smell of puke to be hanging in the air, but it had been cleaned up as well, and the dominant smell in the room was the scent of disinfectant.

But Isabelle Thorndale was there, standing in front of her prized painting, and right behind her was Mr. Sokolov, as if he was waiting his turn in line.

As Isabelle turned to speak to the little man, she saw me. Her annoyance was obvious. "What is she doing here?"

"I called her," Valerie lied.

"Why?"

"Mother, whether you like it or not, this is a big story. You can let the police spin their version and let the rumor mill go wild, *or* you can control the narrative. Make sure we tell *our* side of the story."

Isabelle frowned. "That's not a completely terrible idea. At least she's not wearing that godforsaken outfit."

Mr. Sokolov cleared his throat. "Ma'am? Do you mind if I take a look?"

"I just looked at it," she said. "It doesn't look damaged."

"That's good, but I'd like to examine it myself."

Isabelle stepped aside, and Sokolov folded his hands behind his back and leaned forward like there was a hinge at his waist. He stayed in this position, practically motionless, for a full minute. Finally his head jerked upward and spun around, his eyes so big they seemed to fill up his little glasses entirely.

"Did you find damage?" Isabelle asked, alarm clear in her voice.

"No," he said weakly. I noticed the bead of sweat that had appeared on his forehead. "No damage at all."

"Then what's the problem?"

Sokolov pointed at the painting. "The problem is . . . this painting is a fake!"

"A fake?" Isabelle screeched. "But that's impossible. You just examined this painting two days ago!"

"No, madam. Two days ago, I examined *a* painting. A genuine Irek Knutsen. One that was in impeccable shape. My appraisal of *that* painting still stands. But *this* is not the same painting. This is a forgery."

* * *

ISABELLE THORNDALE LET LOOSE a series of curse words that would make a truck mechanic queasy. She stormed out of the room, and by the sound of things, began breaking stuff.

Probably very expensive stuff.

Valerie ran after her mother. That left me alone with Mr. Sokolov.

"I don't know anything about paintings," I said, "so I'm curious. How can you tell it's a fake?"

"Now that I'm looking for it, it's obvious, but at first, not so much. I was only interested to see if there was any blood splatter or anything like that. I wasn't looking *at* the painting so much as *on* the painting. But once I noticed it . . . well, like I said, it was obvious."

"What was obvious?"

"The brushstroke patterns."

"They're not the same as in the original?"

"That's just it. They are the same—but not the way you think. It really is a *very* good forgery. A good forger uses the same style, the same materials, the same brushstrokes. But a forger will never be the original artist, which means the brushstrokes can never *really* be natural. Not to a trained eye like mine."

"You seem impressed."

"Impressed? No. The theft of an original Irek Knutsen is going to cost someone an awful lot of money. In fact, it's going to cost *me* a hefty brokerage commission. So, no, that doesn't impress me."

"Wait—brokerage commission? Was Mrs. Thorndale going to sell the painting?"

Sokolov was about to answer, then caught himself. "Excuse me." He took out his cell phone and walked past me and out of the room.

I looked at this odd little painting and had the same thought I had the first time I saw it. *It's just a guy on a horse.* Sure, he was a cowboy, and sure, the horse was bucking him off, but I'd seen plenty of pictures that sort of looked like that. The cloudy blur of bright yellow behind the man and horse didn't make it any better. The thing wasn't even that big. It was about the size of a laptop, give or take a few inches.

And yet, inexplicably, it was worth ten million dollars. "Maybe more," Sokolov had said.

Except it wasn't worth ten million dollars. Not this one. This one was a fake. So basically, there were two virtually identical paintings—both of them terrible—and one was worth ten million dollars while the other was worth . . . nothing.

This was the nothing one.

I agreed with that evaluation.

Which meant, someone had stolen the real Knutsen. And it wasn't some spur-of-the-moment crime of opportunity. Sokolov said this forgery was pretty good. I took that to mean, not the type of thing you could do with a YouTube tutorial in the middle of the night. This crime took planning. This was a heist.

A heist that had turned deadly.

My big story had just gotten a lot bigger.

"You can't be here, Hope."

I spun around to see Sheriff Alex Kramer. He looked exhausted.

"You don't look so good."

"I haven't slept in a while."

"So go home—take a nap."

"I'd very much like to, but I just received a phone call from a hysterical Isabelle Thorndale accusing me of stealing her precious Knutsen."

"And did you confess?"

"What are you doing here, Hope?"

"I feel like we've been over this numerous times. I'm a reporter. This is a big story. I'm doing my investigation."

"I need you to get out of here so I can do my job."

"So, you admit that it's hard to concentrate when I'm around?"

His cheeks flushed. "What? No, that's not what I'm saying at all. You can't be here. You're a civilian."

"I'm a newspaper reporter who recently solved two murders. If you let me stay, I promise to solve this case for you as well."

"You really think insulting me is the best approach?"

"To be honest, I don't really think too hard about the stuff that comes out of my mouth. I have a sort of 'shoot first, ask questions later' sort of mouth. Come on, Sheriff. Please?"

He folded his arms. "No."

"What if I let you beat me in trap shooting next time?"

"In that case . . . hell, no." Not for the first time, he grabbed me by the arm and escorted me out of the room, through the foyer, and outside.

"For real, Hope. I've got a job to do, and you need to let me do it. When my investigation is complete, you can cover the story all you want."

That's when Isabelle Thorndale came striding toward us, screaming. "*Where is my painting?* Sheriff, I need answers!"

"I don't have any."

"How do you plan to find my painting?"

"Did you have it insured?"

"Of course."

"Then call the insurance company. They have investigators who do this sort of thing. I'm a little preoccupied with your dead butler."

"Oh, quit waving the dead butler in my face like I'm supposed to feel bad. I want my painting back, and I want it back *now*."

"I obviously don't know where it is."

"Then *look* for it! Search my house. I don't care. Just find it!"

As Isabelle stormed off, I saw that Alex was clenching his fists. "I can't possibly search every square inch of this place by myself," he grumbled.

"Well . . ." I said. "Maybe you don't have to do it by yourself."

CHAPTER 15

It appeared that my persistence and the sheriff's lack of sleep were the right combination to wear him down. After a few moments spent softly cursing to himself, he took out his phone, called Katie, and told her he needed her help too. Fifteen minutes later, she arrived, and he gave each of us our own pair of latex gloves, plastic evidence bags, and instructions.

"Okay, ladies. Now, thankfully we don't need to get a warrant because Mrs. Thorndale wants her painting back and has given us permission to search every square inch of the premises. But we still have some procedures to follow. And the first rule of conducting a search is—"

"You do not talk about Fight Club?" I interrupted.

He closed his eyes and gave a little frustrated shake of the head.

"I think that's the second rule, too," Katie whispered to me, grinning.

"No," the sheriff said. "The first rule is that you treat everything like evidence and everything with suspicion."

I raised my hand.

"You don't have to raise your hand, Hope. It's just the three of us."

"Do I salute?"

"I'm about ready to not let you help."

"Okay, just one more question. Do I get to carry a badge and gun?"

"Is she always this much of a pain?" he asked Katie.

"Usually more."

Alex explained how he wanted to divide up the house, then he sent us off with one last piece of advice.

"Please don't make me regret this."

Katie and I began our search in the grand living room under the watchful eyes of Valerie Thorndale and Mrs. Scratchett. We dug under couch cushions, lifted up the rug, peered into planters. I opened the little door at the bottom of the stately grandfather clock, and we even pulled paintings away from the walls to see if maybe something was attached to the backs.

Nothing.

We continued like this through much of the main floor. To be honest, it was boring work, reminding me of the house painting I was trying very hard to avoid back at Granny's. But at least I was doing it with Katie. That meant I got to make lots of smart-alecky comments, and she got to rib me about how big my butt had gotten. You know, girl talk.

And all the while, Valerie and Mrs. Scratchett monitored us closely. Either they were curious about what we might find, or they were *worried* about what we might find.

I couldn't tell which.

Our search eventually took us down a back hall to a thick wooden door. I opened it up only to find a cramped narrow staircase leading downward. It instantly made me think of a castle, and I felt certain we were going to find a dungeon at the bottom filled with iron maidens and other devices of torture.

Instead, we found Mrs. Schneider frosting a sheet cake at a large metal industrial worktable in the middle of a huge kitchen. Flour was sprinkled around the table, and some had spread to her gray dress and white apron.

"Excuse us, Mrs. Schneider, but we have to conduct a search of the kitchen."

"Oh? No worries," she said. "I'm just finishing up some work."

I looked through the bottom cupboards while Katie went through stacks of pots and pans. Underneath the sink, I found two large coffee cans filled with lard, and several mouse traps. Yuck on both accounts. Then Katie went through the drawers while I rummaged through the industrial fridge and freezer.

"I assume you'll be going through my room as well?" Mrs. Schneider asked. She put down her spatula and wiped her hands on her apron.

"Actually, if you could show us the way to the staff bedrooms, that'd be great."

She smiled. "Follow me."

She led us out a thick wooden door into a narrow hallway. It was rather drab, and again reminded me of a dungeon. This basement level was obviously strictly for servants.

At a T-intersection, she stopped and gestured. "My room's down this way, and Molly's is the other way."

"Molly?" Katie asked.

"Sorry. Mrs. Scratchett."

We walked to her room first, she opened the door, and we followed her inside. It was small, no more than twelve or thirteen foot square. A closed door probably led to a bathroom, and an open door revealed a tiny closet. There were no windows. A small dresser snugged against the wall just to our left, with a sink beside it. Books were stacked up on a nightstand next to a small, neatly made bed.

"Anything particular you're looking for?"

"Other than a murder weapon and a very stupid painting?"

"Yes, other than that."

"No, that's about it."

Katie searched the dresser drawers while I looked under the bed, then under the mattress, then under the pillows. I moved on to Mrs. Schneider's nightstand. Her taste in books apparently tended toward romance and mystery. Both of us went through her closet, and together we looked in her small bathroom, which held only a stand-up shower and a toilet.

"Watch this," Katie said. "I saw this on a cop show. This is where they always find dope." She lifted the lid to the toilet's water tank.

Her face fell. "I was really hoping for a couple kilos," she said.

I patted her on the back. "A girl can only dream."

"Is that all?" Mrs. Schneider asked.

"In terms of the search, yes. But I was wondering if you might answer a couple questions."

"I don't see why not."

"What did you think of Mr. Pimsey?"

"Are we being honest?"

"The man is dead, so I hope so."

"I didn't care for him much."

"Really?"

"Yes, really."

"Why?"

"He wasn't a very nice man."

"In what way?" Katie asked.

"In the normal way."

"Did you dislike him enough to kill him?" I asked.

She looked up and to her right, like she was thinking about it. Then finally she leveled her eyes with mine. "Under the right circumstances, yes."

"Wait. For real?" Katie said.

"Mrs. Schneider, are you saying you killed Mr. Pimsey?" I asked.

"Of course not. I didn't kill that old fool. I'm just saying that under the right circumstances, I might have." She narrowed her eyes at me. "But I didn't."

"Did anybody else share your opinion of Mr. Pimsey?"

"I'd say most people. He was a difficult man. The only person people liked less was Mrs. Thorndale."

"Can you think of anybody in particular who might have wanted him dead?"

"Dead? I shouldn't think so. Well . . ." She chewed on her lip.

"Well, what?"

"As I mentioned yesterday, I suppose Mrs. Thorndale could do it. Last year, she threw a vase at his head. Luckily, her aim is terrible. Otherwise, who knows?"

Mrs. Schneider went back to her kitchen, and we walked down the hall to where Mrs. Scratchett was now waiting outside her room.

"Come to see how the other half lives, eh?"

She opened her door, and I was instantly struck by how disgusting her room was. Clothes were strewn all over the floor, along with an empty pizza box. The sheets on her bed were rumpled up into a ball, and a definite funk hung in the air.

"Did someone say you're the maid?" Katie asked.

"Hey, *you* try cleaning up for a bunch of brats all day and then see if you've got the energy to clean your own room."

Katie tilted her head. "I know exactly where you're coming from."

"Katie," I said, "maybe you want to search the bed this time?"

"I haven't had my tetanus renewed, so that's a negative."

"Fine."

I carefully lowered myself to my stomach and looked under Mrs. Scratchett's bed. The funk was much worse down here, and as I used the light on my phone to look more closely, I suddenly understood why. There was a very old half-eaten bowl of what might once have been cereal, but was now a white-and-gray moldy sludge. I resisted the urge to gag, then popped to my feet.

"You have an old bowl of cereal under your bed?"

"Maybe. What's your point?"

"That doesn't gross you out?"

Mrs. Scratchett dropped to the floor, stretched her arm under the bed, snatched the moldy cereal, and stood. "Listen, honey," she said. "My dad made me skin and clean a deer when I was only six. It takes more than old dairy to gross me out."

We searched through Mrs. Scratchett's room just like we had with Mrs. Schneider's. Under the mattress, under the rug, inside the closet. We even looked under the toilet tank lid again.

"Still no kilos," Katie groused.

"It's just not your lucky day," I said.

I was lifting an old bra from the corner of her bathroom sink when I found a small picture. It was of Mrs. Scratchett dressed in her maid uniform beside a man in khaki trousers, a khaki work shirt, and a green baseball cap. He looked like he'd lost his teeth. She looked happy.

"Who's this, Mrs. Scratchett?"

She sighed, took the photo from my hands, and gave it a long, soulful look. "That is my Rexy."

"Husband?"

She shook her head.

"Boyfriend?"

She shrugged. "Once upon a time . . ."

"You break up?"

"More like, we were broken up."

"What happened?"

"Walter Pimsey happened." She finally tore her eyes from the photo. "His name was Rex Buttman. He worked here for the Thorndales. He was the gardener before Juan.

Around here, everyone just called him 'Buttman.' Except me. He was my Sexy Rexy."

In addition to missing his teeth, one of Rex's eyes appeared to be permanently closed. I was guessing Scratchett and I had different ideas of what made a man sexy.

"So, you talk about him in the past. Did he die?"

"Oh, God, no. He left. Forced out. Pimsey said our relationship was making both of us too distracted—but Rex in particular. And then one day, he told Rex it was time to move on. I couldn't believe it. Still, I thought Rex could get another job somewhere around here. But he wasn't having any of it. He got a job on a fishing boat off the coast of Alaska. Invited me to join him. But . . . I just couldn't."

"How long ago was that?"

"Five years."

"That must have made you pretty angry at Pimsey."

"I'll stop you right there. I wanted to wring his perfect little English neck when that all happened, but I don't want to now. I am not your killer. No matter how many questions you ask me."

"So, who *did* kill Pimsey?"

"That's what the sheriff is supposed to find out."

"But if you had to guess?"

"Nobody. That's my guess."

"C'mon, Mrs. Scratchett, surely you have a guess. Who would be most likely?"

"Most likely? Well, that's easier. Mrs. Thorndale would be most likely. She's meaner than a hornet, and she and Pimsey have been after each other forever."

"I've got one more question."

"Shoot."

"You're the one who cleans and dusts everything. Whoever killed Pimsey used a dense and heavy object to do it. Have you noticed anything missing that could have been used as the murder weapon?"

"I've actually been thinking about that—but no, I haven't noticed anything."

"Okay. Well, I guess that's it. We're supposed to search Valerie's room next. Any chance you could show us?"

She smiled. "Follow me."

CHAPTER 16

Mrs. Scratchett led us back up to the first floor and to the house's front entrance just as Sheriff Kramer and Juan walked in.

"Hello, Miss Walker," Juan said with a smile.

"Hey, Juan." I nodded at Alex. "Sheriff."

"Learn anything?" Alex asked me.

"Yeah. Don't go into Mrs. Scratchett's room without a decontamination suit."

He gave me a confused look.

"Don't ask. How about you?"

"Juan here has the most organized machine shed in the history of mankind. But other than that, no. Now I'm headed upstairs to the men's bedrooms."

"We'll join you. We still need to look at the Thorndale women's stuff."

Mrs. Scratchett, Alex, and Katie started up the grand staircase to the second floor. Bringing up the rear, Juan tapped me on the shoulder.

"I meant to ask. Have you had any chance to look into April?"

"I'm sorry, Juan. With everything going on . . ."

He nodded. "I know, I know. It's just—what can I say? I'm worried."

"Like I said, I promise I'll look into it. Just give me a little more time."

When we reached the top of the stairs, Alex strode down the hall toward a rather impatient-looking Clay Thorndale, and Mrs. Scratchett and Juan went their own way. Valerie was waiting for me and Katie beside her own bedroom door.

She shook her head and rolled her eyes. "Let's get this over with."

Her room was more than twice as big as the servants' rooms downstairs. It held a solid oak queen-sized bed with a white gold-trimmed comforter and plenty of overstuffed pillows, a comfortable chair beside a small table and a television, a walk-in closet, and an en suite bathroom.

"Not bad," Katie said. "You ever Airbnb this thing?"

"Yeah, Valerie. How much time do you even spend here?" I asked.

She shrugged. "I've got an apartment in Boise, but I make it to Hopeless when I can."

"I hope you don't mind me asking," Katie said, "but do you work? Do you have some sort of trust fund?"

Valerie laughed. "I don't mind. Once upon a time, I had a small trust fund. We all did. And we all did the same thing with it—we blew right through it. And I made the very unfortunate mistake of blowing through that money while married to a lazy artist. When the divorce was settled, he and his lawyer argued—very persuasively, according to the judge—that I was the one who supported us during our marriage, and therefore I owed him spousal support."

"Yikes."

"Yes, yikes. To be honest, I didn't prepare for the real world very well. I guess I thought I was just going to be a Thorndale. I thought that would be enough."

"I take it, it wasn't."

"Not by a long shot. I bounced around from job to job until finally I figured out that I knew a hell of a lot about wine. I carved out a niche as the sommelier at a fancy restaurant in Boise. Eventually I found a partner, and we opened up a restaurant. And now that one restaurant has become three restaurants."

"Wow. That's impressive. A classic riches-to-rags-to-riches story."

"Not back to riches . . . but yes, out of the rags. It's hard work, though—exhausting. Still, when I get free days, I come to Hopeless. My mother's not the easiest woman in the world, but she's still my mother."

I thought about my own mother, and wondered where she was. I still hated her for leaving so many years ago. But like Valerie said, she was still my mother. And if I had a chance to see her one more time, I wouldn't miss that opportunity for the world.

Katie and I searched Valerie's room. We didn't find any mold farms under the bed, and generally had a much better time than we had with Molly Scratchett. Katie insisted on searching the bathroom, and I caught her snuggling her face against Valerie's thick plush towels, mumbling, "As soft as a baby's bottom."

When we were finished, I asked Valerie the same thing I'd asked everyone.

"Did you like Pimsey?"

She folded her arms. "Yes."

"You sound unsure."

"Pimsey, like everyone in this house, was complicated. But I liked him, unequivocally."

"You didn't kill him?"

"No, I did not." She said it matter-of-factly, with little emotion.

"So, who did?"

"I've given that a lot of thought. And I can't believe I'm saying this, but I think Mrs. Scratchett might have done it."

"Why do you say that?"

"First, she's rough. I'm not sure killing a man would upset her too much."

"And second?"

"She was in love with a man Pimsey fired. I don't think I could forgive someone for doing something like that."

We finished up in Valerie's room and stepped out into the hall. Kitty's room was next in line. "Does Kitty want to be here while we search her room?" I asked Valerie.

"She won't care. Trust me." She walked us down the hall.

Kitty's room was nothing like Valerie's. It was more like a scene from *Orange Is the New Black*. A twin bed on a white metal frame. A small bookcase with five books on it. A closet. A bathroom. Both empty.

Katie clapped her hands together. "Search complete. Now *that's* my type of police work."

"What gives, Valerie? Kitty doesn't come home much?"

"Hardly ever. She lives in Boise, like me. She visits occasionally, but never stays at the house."

"Why?"

"She and Mother don't see eye to eye on things."

"Which things?"

"All the things. Kitty didn't go the college Mother wanted. She didn't study the things Mother wanted. And she never, *ever* dated the men Mother wanted."

"What kind of men did your mother want?"

Valerie shrugged. "Businessmen. Finance. Respectable family. Plenty of money. And most importantly, her own age. Kitty's got a thing for older men. Always has. Freaks Mother out."

"And what does Kitty do for a living?"

"I'm honestly not sure. I know she teaches yoga. She did some community theater back in the day. She waited tables at one point. But now . . . who knows? Her apartment's just half a mile from mine, but we hardly see each other."

"Sounds warm."

"It's not."

"Since Kitty's not here, I'll ask you. Did she like Pimsey?"

Valerie nodded. "Yes."

"Wow," Katie said. "That's the first time we've gotten that answer. Pimsey was apparently not a very likable guy."

"I don't understand it," Valerie said. "But ever since she

was little, she took to him. I think it's because they both suffered so much punishment from my mother. Maybe they felt like they were on the same team."

"Could Kitty have done something like this?"

"Killed Pimsey? Why would she? She might kill Mother. But Pimsey? No."

Valerie walked us down to our last stop—Isabelle Thorndale's bedroom.

Even the door told us this room was more important than the others. It was larger. Made of thick quarter-sawn oak, possibly hewn from a single trunk. When Valerie knocked on it, it practically resonated.

"Come in!" Isabelle shouted.

The room was huge. It had to be to hold all the antique furniture. The bed alone was a monstrosity, an old brass four-poster that looked like something out of a gothic cathedral. Giant wardrobes, bookcases, and carved chests of drawers lined the walls. Everything looked like it came from a different age. An age of . . . gentility. And wealth. The only modern touch was a flat-screen television affixed to the wall opposite the bed.

Across the room, two stiff upholstered chairs stood on either side of a potted fern. Isabelle was seated in one chair, her hands folded in her lap, her legs crossed at the ankles, like she might be posing for a painting.

"Hello, Mrs. Thorndale."

She stood. "Miss Walker." She narrowed her gaze at Katie. "Who's this?"

Katie shot out her hand. "Katie Rodgers, professional breastfeeder. Nice to make your acquaintance, ma'am."

Now Isabelle narrowed her gaze at me. "Where'd you find this idiot?"

"Under a table in kindergarten. She was crying. It was kind of pathetic. Even for a five-year-old."

Katie turned to me, hands on her hips. "I've told you, I had seasonal allergies as a kid. Why you gotta make it seem like I was a big baby?"

I pinched her cheek and squeezed. "Even back then, you had adorable cheeks."

She knocked my hand off. "You're dead, Hope Walker. Dead."

"I hate to break up . . . whatever *this* is," Isabelle said with contempt, "but you are in my room and you are wasting my time. Now get on with your search or get the hell out of here!"

So that's what we did. By this point, Katie and I had our routine down pat. We looked under the bed, behind cushions, through clothing drawers, behind cabinets. The only thing I didn't do was take a knife to her pillows and rip them apart. I'd seen that move a couple times in the movies and I would so love to do that. Maybe Katie and I could sneak into Gemima's house sometime and do a number on her pillows?

I shook my head. A girl could only dream.

But once again, we came up with nothing. No murder weapon. No painting. Nothing particularly suspicious.

And then I got to Isabelle Thorndale's nightstand. A half full bottle of Jim Beam whiskey stood beside a variety of pill bottles. I shot Isabelle a look, and she shot one right back.

"It's my nightly regimen. How else am I supposed to live forever?"

Part of me thought she might not be joking.

I opened the nightstand drawer. Inside was a small picture of her and her husband along with a little girl—probably Valerie. The photo was old and worn down by time. Next to it was an old leather journal with a band around it. I pulled it out, loosened the band, and started to page through it.

"Put that down!" Isabelle snapped.

"Sorry, Mrs. Thorndale. I'm doing a search."

"You're searching for my Knutsen, and I assure you it is not inside that book!" She advanced on me and tried to yank the book out of my hands, but I wouldn't let go.

"I'm doing a search on behalf of the sheriff," I said.

She gritted her teeth and moved her face closer to mine. "A search that I am allowing. *So far*. You have no search warrant, Miss Walker. This book has nothing to do with my missing painting."

"Why don't you let the sheriff be the judge of that?"

"Are you some kind of imbecile? You're here to find my painting, not to nose around in my personal business, Miss . . . Nosy." She ripped the book out of my hands, spun around, and stormed out of the room.

Katie and I exchanged a look.

"Miss Nosy?" Katie said. "That's the best she's got?"

"Think she's hiding something?" I asked.

"Everybody's hiding something."

As we left Isabelle Thorndale's room, shouting sounded from down the hall. Mortimer Snoot stepped out of one of the bedrooms, screaming his head off. It was easy to see why. His hands were behind his back. Cuffed. And behind him stood Sheriff Alex Kramer.

When Alex saw us, he just gave us an exhausted shake of his head. He held something up in his gloved right hand. It was one of those big Maglite flashlights, the kind that police and security often use. And when I took a closer look, I saw something else.

It was covered in blood.

CHAPTER 17

Mortimer Snoot had hidden the murder weapon inside his mattress. Or at least, that's where Alex found it. He'd first noticed the duct tape on the underside of the mattress, and when he asked Snoot about it, Snoot just shrugged. Must have been a rip in the mattress, he said. But Alex peeled the tape off, and when he did, the bloody flashlight fell out.

Some tests would need to be done, but it seemed likely this was the murder weapon.

"Seems pretty clear-cut to me," Alex said.

Katie smiled. "Lock him up and throw away the key so I can get out of here. There's a very tall glass of wine with my name on it at home. Seriously, I write my name on the wine glasses. The bottles, too. Sometimes I also write, 'Chris, keep your hands off!'"

Isabelle sneered. "Lock him up? That's too good for a scumbag like him. You should just shoot him. You can do that, right, Sheriff?"

"I'm afraid that's not how it works, Mrs. Thorndale," Alex said.

"Ah, right, you're a lawman. A hanging is more your thing. I wouldn't mind watching a good hanging. But not before he tells me where my Knutsen is. Out with it, Snoot!"

"I don't *know* where your painting is," Snoot cried. "I didn't do it, Mrs. Thorndale. I didn't do any of this!"

Isabelle looked at me. "Miss Walker, I hear you're pretty handy with your foot. Could you kick him in the balls until he talks?"

Alex held out a hand to stop me before I could even decide whether to take Isabelle up on her suggestion. "Hope, you will do nothing of the sort. Mrs. Thorndale, we do not torture people, nor do we hang people. We collect evidence, we present the evidence at trial, a jury forms a verdict, and a judge hands down a sentence. That's how it works."

"Seems like a grossly inefficient system, if you ask me," Isabelle said. "Give me a hammer and five minutes alone with this turd and I bet we could cut through a lot of red tape."

Alex, surprisingly patient, set out to explain the subtle legalese behind why you can't beat suspects with hammers.

As for me, I felt like I should be glad the case was solved. After all, I had things to do—like spying on teenage girls and painting old houses. But something didn't seem right. Snoot was a buffoon, there was no doubt about that. But a murderer?

That's when I remembered the little note. The one I

had conveniently decided not to share with the newest sheriff of Hopeless. I was fairly certain that whoever had killed Pimsey felt bad about it. So bad that they hand-delivered a note under the door of the Library the morning after the murder.

I pulled the note from my back pocket, unfolded it, and read it again.

I didn't mean to do it.

It was an apology of sorts. An admission of guilt. A confession.

I charged past Alex and into Snoot's room. I immediately spotted what I was hoping to find—a small desk. I riffled through the papers in the first drawer and came up with an unfinished handwritten letter that Snoot had been composing to someone. Perfect.

By this point, Sheriff Kramer had come in the room behind me, and he was doing that thing where you're just about to start yelling at someone but you're trying to hold it together.

"Hope! What the heck are you doing?"

I compared the handwriting on the letter to the handwriting on the note. I was sure I would discover they didn't match.

I was wrong.

The handwriting was the same.

Earl Denton called me at seven the next morning. "How's the story about Mrs. Thorndale's party coming along?"

"Yeah, funny thing about that story."

"Hope, you'd better be working on it. That old bat's money is the only thing keeping us in business."

"Wait. You really haven't heard?"

"Heard what? I've been on a cruise ship for the last two days."

"There was another murder."

My news surprised Earl so much that I'm pretty sure he shot his dentures out of his mouth. I heard a thoomp, followed by another thoomp, followed by what sounded like Earl and his wife frantically scrambling around to get his teeth back. When he finally returned to the phone, I had to ask.

"Are you okay, Earl?"

"I am. But all the people who just watched me and my wife roll around the deck of the ship looking for my false teeth probably aren't. Did you say there was another murder?"

I told Earl the whole story.

"Well," he said, "seems to me if this Snoot feller is to blame, you can go ahead and run the story."

"There's just one little problem."

"What's that?"

"I'm not so sure he did it."

"You said yourself this guy's a total creep."

"That's right. And he is. But a criminal mastermind? Listen, this guy falls somewhere between Gomer Pyle and Barney Fife on the competence scale."

"That bad, huh? Well, so what? That would explain why he did such a poor job of hiding the murder weapon. Anyone with half a brain wouldn't hide it in their own room."

"Honestly, that's part of the reason why I don't suspect him. How could someone be smart enough to traffic in art theft, but dumb enough to do that? And then there's the note slipped under the Library door. It just feels . . ."

"Wrong," Earl said.

"Yes."

"You got any other leads?"

"Not really."

"Then I suggest you find some."

* * *

EARL WAS RIGHT. I needed some new leads. I needed some new evidence.

Unfortunately, there was something else I had promised to do, and I'd been ignoring it for too long. I looked at the blue ink on my hand. At the reminder I had written to myself.

April.

Juan's niece.

A murder was a much bigger deal than a depressed high school girl. But I'd already turned Juan away twice, and I didn't feel good about it. He clearly cared about April like she was his own daughter—and he was just as clearly very concerned about her. Making a few calls was the least I could do.

I dialed the number of my old high school and left a

message for Mrs. Hamilton. When she called me back, I explained the nature of my call. She invited me to come by her room at lunch.

That meant I had some time to kill.

I thought about going out and finding some of those leads Earl was talking about. *Then* I thought about how good it would feel to go back to bed and sleep for another two hours. That seemed like an easy choice.

But when my phone buzzed with a text message from Bess—*Granny says that house ain't gonna paint itself*—I sighed and found myself going for Option C.

When I got to Granny's, I found four gallons of new white exterior house paint and three new paintbrushes waiting for me at the base of the ladder—which was already fully extended and in the ready position. Beneath the paintbrushes was a pink Post-It note with a smiley face drawn on it.

I promptly gave that smiley face the middle finger.

I spent the next three miserable hours of my life back on top of that ladder, painting away at the house of my youth. I knew there was no way I would be able to finish on time, but hey, at least I was trying.

At eleven thirty, I drove back to the Library, took a shower, and threw on dark jeans, a white top, and a light jacket. I put my hair in a ponytail and drove to Hopeless Senior High.

Like pretty much everything I'd done since my return to Hopeless, this was a reunion of sorts.

In high school, I was a real pain in the rump. For a lot of people. Granny, of course. Sheriff Kline. And my teachers. But still, I was a pretty decent student. And when it came to English and journalism, I was a teacher's dream.

At the front desk, I received a visitor's tag from a secretary I'd never met. Once upon a time, Katie and I let the air out of the tires of a secretary who had tattled on us for leaving school early. I was happy she was no longer here.

I found Mrs. Hamilton in the art room, cleaning some brushes in the sink.

"You must be Hope. I'm Bev Hamilton."

"It's nice to meet you, Mrs. Hamilton."

"Please. Call me Bev. I get 'Mrs. Hamilton'ed all day long."

She dried her hands, sat down at one of the tables, and gestured for me to do the same. "I hope you don't mind, but I called Juan just to make sure it was all right to speak with you. I take it you and Juan are friends?"

"Actually, we just met. But I think he figures since I'm a reporter, maybe I'll have more luck than him."

"With what, exactly?"

"He's worried about April. He said she kind of shut down near the end of last year, and hasn't been the same. Distracted, moody . . . you know the drill."

"This *is* a high school girl we're talking about," Mrs. Hamilton said.

"That's what I told him, but he insisted there's more to it. And when he asked her about it, she shut down even more. He said the two of you are close?"

"She's a nice girl, and a brilliant artist."

"She's pretty good?"

She gave me a look. "Not pretty good. She's incredible.

Come here."

Bev led me to a corner where a bunch of canvases leaned against the wall. She went to one particular stack of four and turned them around to face forward, lined up side by side.

The first was of a teenage girl with her hand running through a mess of tangled frizzy black hair. She looked deep in thought, but there was a twinkle in her eye.

"This one's a self-portrait," Bev said.

"It's mesmerizing."

"I know, right?"

The next one was a desert landscape. Simple and gorgeous.

"She did that one too?"

Mrs. Hamilton nodded.

The next canvas was the largest, and drawn from the perspective of the sky looking down on a crowd below. Everyone in the crowd was looking up, and the detail on the faces was astonishing. Their expressions held a mixture of fear and hope. It made me want to know what they were looking at.

The last painting showed a woman and a little girl walking along a set of train tracks, holding hands. The woman appeared to be . . . fading away.

"These are incredible," I said.

"I told you."

"And I don't know anything about painting, but they're nothing alike."

"I know. She's still searching for her style. But in the ten years I've been doing this, she's the best student I've had."

"Okay, she can paint. But is she happy?"

"Were you happy in high school?"

"Sometimes."

She laughed. "Me too." She folded her arms and tilted her head in thought. "I'd say she's not as happy as other kids, but she's an artist. She keeps a lot of things inside. And of course, there's boys."

"Any particular boy?"

"I think so."

"Juan didn't say anything about that."

"Hardly the first adult not to know what a teenager was up to."

"Good point. Juan says she started acting differently at the end of the last school year. Any chance that could coincide with this boy?"

"Um . . . maybe. I guess."

"Does he have a name?"

"She's never told me about him, if that's what you're getting at. But she's on the phone more—steps away, out into the hall, that kind of thing."

"His name?" I asked again.

"I think it's Carlos. I saw a call come in one time when her phone was on the table."

"Do you know of any Carlos in school?"

"I don't think there is one."

"Could it be a nickname?"

Bev shrugged. "Anything's possible."

"Okay, so this could be about a boy. Does she seem happy when she steps away to use the phone? Love can twist anyone in knots. You think April's in love?"

"In love? I don't think so. I guess, now that I think about it . . . she seems . . . concerned."

"And you have no idea what it's about?"

"I don't. But she's a good kid. I don't think she's in trouble."

Perhaps, I thought. *Then again, she's a teenage girl.*

* * *

I LEFT school debating whether to try to find some new leads, or suck it up and go back to work on Granny's house. Once again, I settled for Option C. This time it rhymed with Sour Cream & Onion Pringles.

Ten minutes later, I was sitting in my car, in front of the Library, one can of Pringles and one thirty-two-ounce Diet Coke richer. It was a glorious meal, and I hated myself with every bite. I was wondering if I should tip the can upside down to get the last little Pringle crumbs when my phone rang. It was Katie.

"Hey," I said.

"What are you doing?"

"Eating a healthy salad and some lean protein?"

"You're eating chips, aren't you?"

"How did you know?"

"I can smell chips through the phone."

"What are you, a superhero?"

"Told you I'm not a sidekick. I think I was bitten by a radioactive Dorito in high school."

"So, what's up?" I asked. "Has Snoot confessed yet?"

"He claims he's innocent. Keeps shaking the bars to his

cell and crying. I told him if he keeps it up, I'll let my children spend the rest of the day with him. But I didn't call you to talk about boring stuff like murder. I've got much better news."

"*Magic Mike 3* just went straight to video?"

Unexpected silence. Followed by stammering. "W-w-wait. There's a *Magic Mike 3*?"

"Just trying to distract you. You're like a cat with a laser pointer. Too easy."

"So, is there a *Magic Mike 3* or not?"

"Focus, sister."

"You can't joke about *Magic Mike*. That's sacred territory."

"Moving along . . ."

"Okay, I've got good news. Are you sitting down?"

"You do realize that sitting down is what you do with news that *isn't* good."

"You're right. It's not good. It's great. I've just solved a big problem."

"Good for you."

"No. Good for *you*."

Uh-oh.

"Katie, what are you talking about?"

"What thing have you not done in the last twelve years?"

That would include quite a number of things. But I knew Katie—and I had a bad feeling about where this was going.

"Katie, you're scaring me. What have you done?"

"The kind of thing a best friend does. Hope Walker, I just got you a date."

CHAPTER 18

I think I went through the first three stages of grief in a verbal tirade that lasted at least three minutes and included two dozen bleep-worthy words. All Katie did in response was laugh and say this was good for me.

I didn't believe that for one second, but as I rounded third base toward depression, I was at least curious who she had in mind.

"So here I was, listening to Mortimer Snoop make noises like a stuck pig when who should come by the sheriff's office but Clay Thorndale."

"Clay? You set me up with Clay?"

"He wanted your contact info, and I asked him why. He said he wanted to take you out on a date."

"And what did you do?"

"I told him you would *love* to go on a date with him and I gave him your cell."

"But—but why would you *do* that?"

"Isn't it obvious? You need to get back in the game, girl."

"I don't even like him," I said.

"You don't have to like him. You just have to go out with him."

"Oh, nice. Is that what you'll tell Lucy someday?"

"Lucy will never go twelve years without an actual date. Nope, this is advice I save for my big loser friends."

"But Clay? I think he's an alcoholic."

"Maybe. But there's an attractive and charming guy in there somewhere."

"I saw him puke all over Mrs. Thorndale's floor."

"So, you've already had an icebreaker. Even better."

"Katie, I can't do this."

"Yes, Hope. You can."

Then she hung up on me. She actually hung up on me. I was about to phone her back when my cell buzzed. An unknown number. I answered it.

It was Clay Thorndale.

He asked me to dinner. I said yes. I didn't even know what I was doing. This had all happened so fast, and I was out of practice.

When he asked where we should go, I regrouped. "Meet me at the Library at seven," I said.

And before he could disagree, I hung up.

Then I called Katie back.

"Clay Thorndale called."

"How'd it go?"

"Better than I thought. We've got a date for tomorrow."

She squealed in delight.

"But I was thinking . . . maybe you and I could get together tonight."

"Can't tonight. Gotta make dinner for the kids."

"Perfect," I said. "It's kids-eat-free night at the Library."

* * *

AT SIX THIRTY THAT NIGHT, Katie showed up at the dartboard with a very annoyed look on her face.

"Granny just told me there is no kids-eat-free night tonight."

"Not true," I said, and pointed to scores of crushed peanut shells all over the barroom floor. "It's all-you-can-eat peanuts."

"They always serve free peanuts."

I smiled. "I know. Isn't that special?"

"Okay, Hope. To what do I owe this particular deception, and why do you look like you've taken a shower?"

"First off, buy the kids some chicken tenders. I'll pay for it."

"You don't have any money."

"Then you pay for it, and I'll promise to pay you back."

"You're like Mother Teresa."

"More like Dorothy Day. Either way, I need you tonight."

She smiled and rubbed her hands together. "Tell me this involves you kissing a hot guy."

"No!"

Katie gave me a look. "Well, don't make it sound awful."

"Right, not awful. I just meant, it's more important

than that. As much as I'd like to believe Snoot's guilty, it doesn't feel right, and you need to help me sort this through."

"You took a shower just so you and I could hang out and talk about murder and mayhem?"

"Like I always say—clean hair, clean mind."

"You have never said that. No one has ever said that."

"I think it's gonna catch on, though."

She gave me a suspicious look, then went to the bar and ordered food and drinks from Bess. She handed Dominic and Lucy a bunch of quarters and told them to go crazy on the jukebox. Then with Celia in her left arm and two beers in her right hand, she joined me at a table and ripped into some chicken tenders.

"So," I said, "before we talk about the killer, I suggest we start with that stupid painting. Maybe *that's* what we should be focusing on. That art expert from Billingham's said it was a really good forgery. I think it took him a while to figure it out."

Katie let out a breath. "Thank God he wasn't examining the real Knutsen."

"Why?"

"I'd be mortified if they discovered the booger."

"What booger?"

Katie looked around like she was about to share espionage secrets with me and lowered her voice. "It's possible that I took the kids to Mrs. Thorndale's stupid party two years ago."

"Why on earth . . .?"

"Hey, when you've got little kids, you are *desperate* to find things that pass the time. Honestly, you just pray that

God can get you to their next nap before you rip your hair out. And when there's free food involved? Well, that's a double win. Hence why I agreed to come here tonight."

"On account of the free peanuts and all."

"Remind me sometime to tell you how much you suck. So anyway, I decided, against my better judgment, to get in line to see the famous Knutsen. And we *just* get up to the painting when—of course—Dominic lets loose an absolutely enormous sneeze."

"Oh, no . . ."

"Oh, yes. Direct hit. Both nostrils were locked and loaded, and he threw his hips into it for good measure. Blasted that painting like a lawn sprinkler in June. And this sneeze had a little something extra behind it. You know me. Mucus runs deep with my kind."

"I can't believe Dominic boogered the Knutsen."

"Oh, stop. You've met my kids. You believe it. And now, two years later, the scandal is going to catch up with us." Katie looked over at Dominic. He was wrapped around Granny's leg, and she was dragging him around the bar, pretending he wasn't even there. "Enjoy your last night of freedom, my sweet little maniac. We'll never forget you. I'm turning your bedroom into a crafting room."

"You craft?" I said.

"Nah, but once he's in prison, I'll have all this extra time on my hands."

"Hold up on the prison visits just yet, my friend. Remember, the only Knutsen we've got at the moment is a fake."

"Oh, right. Dominic still has time to flee the country."

"Be sure to pack him a healthy lunch. But back to business. Which of our suspects is most capable of running an *Ocean's Eleven* kind of operation?"

"You mean *Ocean's Twelve,* right?"

"No. *Ocean's Twelve* is the sequel."

Katie smiled. "I know. I prefer the sequel."

"That's not even possible. Nobody prefers the sequel."

"But they've got that smoking-hot European master thief. They call him the Night Fox."

"Because George Clooney and Brad Pitt weren't foxy enough for you?"

She shrugged. "What can I say? I've got refined tastes."

As if on cue, Dominic blew an enormous zerbert on Lucy's stomach.

Katie and I looked at each other and burst into laughter.

"But seriously," I said, "other than Snoot, do you have any guesses who might have done it?"

"I think they *all* did it," Katie said, dipping her next chicken finger in ranch. "Don't they all seem a little shifty to you?"

"Okay, no offense, but I'm going to suggest we assume —just for a moment—that they didn't *all* do it."

"Then start at the beginning," Katie said. "What are the facts?"

"Fine. The beginning. Every year, Mrs. Thorndale throws herself an ostentatious party."

"Where they use fancy words like 'ostentatious.'"

"Touché. And every year at this party, she trots out her famous ugly painting for the peasantry of Hopeless to see."

"And sneeze on."

"Correct," I said. "But this year is especially important. She has this Sokolov guy authenticate and appraise the painting the day before the party."

"And he's going to announce the official appraisal at the party."

"Right. Because that's a totally normal thing to do. Meanwhile, the night before the party, Mrs. Thorndale and Pimsey get into a big fight."

Katie jumped in. "Which would not have been all that unusual if he hadn't turned up dead."

"Which he did."

"At the social event of the year! Very inconsiderate of him."

"Very. So at the party, nobody can find Pimsey. And they need him because he's the only person Mrs. Thorndale trusted with a key to that room. So Isabelle Thorndale and her two eldest children, Clay and Valerie, go to the room."

"Along with *Hopeless News*'s most intrepid investigative reporter," Katie said.

"Of course. That woman has a nose for news."

"I hear they call her Miss Nosy."

"Some do. So naturally, she's on the scene when Clay—"

"Your new boyfriend," Katie interjects.

"Shut up. Clay breaks down the locked door, and there on the floor is Pimsey, dead."

"Presumably for some time."

"So it appeared. So, who had opportunity? Who was at the house? Snoot, Scratchett, and Schneider all live there.

Juan works there, but lives in town with his niece. Isabelle Thorndale was home, as were Valerie and Clay. Kitty wasn't there yet. She didn't arrive until just after the body was discovered."

"Well, there's your list of suspects." Katie scratched her chin. "Which one of them did it?"

"The evidence says Snoot."

"And that evidence is mounting."

"What do you mean?" I asked.

"The Maglite," Katie said. "They ran a blood test. Came back B-positive, which matches the type found on Pimsey's donor card."

"So it's definitely the murder weapon."

"One would think," Katie said. "And it has Snoot's fingerprints on it. *And* Snoot has admitted that the Maglite belongs to him, though he claims he has no idea how it got into his mattress."

"You're right. The evidence is mounting."

"But it feels like a setup," Katie said.

"That's interesting . . . Maybe it's not about the painting at all. Maybe it's about getting Snoot in trouble."

Katie frowned. "You're saying someone hates Snoot so much, they're willing to kill someone else just to get him in trouble?"

"He *is* a really creepy dude."

Katie shook her head. "I'm not buying it. I think he's just so clueless, he makes an easy mark."

"Okay. Let's take Snoot off the list. Anybody else you want to scratch off?"

"You said Kitty didn't get there until just after the murder?"

"Right. And Juan lives at home with his niece."

"That leaves Scratchett, Schneider, Mrs. Thorndale, Valerie, and Clay," Katie said. "Five suspects. You got theories about any of them?"

I shrugged. "Scratchett and Schneider seem pretty harmless."

"Looks can be deceiving."

"Right," I said. "And actually, they both came up with a theory about Mrs. Thorndale. They thought that after the fight, maybe Pimsey was so angry, he went down to steal her painting to finally get back at the old bat. She follows him down, sees what he's doing, and bonks him over the head. She can't move him, so she grabs his keys, locks the room, and acts shocked the next day when he's found dead."

Katie leaned back. "That actually makes a lot of sense."

"I know, right? But there are two problems."

"What?"

"First, the murder weapon. Mrs. Thorndale just happened to have Snoot's giant flashlight in her hand?"

"It *was* nighttime," Katie said. "Maybe she needed a flashlight."

"In her own house? I'm pretty sure they have light switches. But more importantly, there's the note shoved under the Library door."

"'I didn't mean to do it,'" Katie said.

"Let's say the old lady *did* do it. Does Mrs. Thorndale strike you as the kind of woman who would drive downtown, get out of her car, and slide a confession note under the door of a bar in some weird hope that a newspaper reporter will find it?"

Katie frowned. “Does that mean Isabelle Thorndale is off the list?”

“No. It just means I’m not sure that the Scratchett-Schneider theory adds up. But the old lady’s definitely hiding something. You saw how she reacted when I opened that journal.”

“Okay. What about Valerie?” Katie asked.

“She seems nice. Normal, even. Nothing really points to her.”

“You think she’d be capable of killing Pimsey?”

“No. But that also means if somehow she did, she definitely would feel bad about it. Bad enough to leave a note . . . maybe.”

“And now let’s talk about Clay,” Katie said, suddenly smiling.

“Right, the man you set me up with. A man who is a suspect in a murder investigation.”

“Hey, beggars can’t be choosy.”

“I’m not begging for a date.”

“I know, and that’s the problem. Honey, it’s been twelve years. You need to move on. I need you to move on. Hell, Jimmy needs you to move on. He called me the other day from heaven.”

“They have phones?”

“Yeah, but it was a collect call.”

“Sounds like Jimmy.”

“And he begged me to make you go on a date with someone. He told me he lights a candle for you every day in church.”

“So now Jimmy’s a regular churchgoer?”

“When in Rome and all.”

"I'm not good at dates," I said.

Katie's face turned gentle. Understanding. She reached out and grabbed my hand. "But you used to be. And you can be again."

"Seriously, though. You set me up on a date with a Thorndale?"

"That's why it's called a date and not a marriage proposal. It's just a start. Just to get you back in the game. Hey, and maybe to spice things up a bit, you can ask him if he killed the butler."

As if on cue, the front door to the Library swung open, and Clay Thorndale walked in. He wore brown tweed pants, a brown sport coat, and a white button-down shirt. His hair was feathered, his face filled with a broad smile. He looked happy.

And like he really didn't belong in Granny's bar.

"Yes," I said. "Maybe I will."

CHAPTER 19

Katie's eyes widened. "Your date with Clay is tonight? Here?"

"Yep. I lied about it being tomorrow."

"*That's* why you bamboozled me into coming."

"That's right. You may have set me up on a date, but that doesn't mean I have to like it. And it sure as hell doesn't mean I'm doing it alone."

"You're weird, Hope Walker. But I still like you. And I get it. Maybe if it's going really badly, just yell out a code word."

"Like what?"

"How about 'homicidal maniac'?"

That made me laugh, which was good, because seeing a man coming toward me for the express purpose of having a date was making me all sorts of nervous.

He smiled as he approached, and reached out to give me a hug. But I fumbled it up by extending a hand for a handshake. I ended up hitting him in the nose, which was not at all what I was aiming for.

"Sorry about that. I . . . um . . . just sorry."

"Don't mention it. So, the Library. I haven't been here since . . . college, I guess. Are you sure you don't want to go someplace . . .?"

"Nicer?"

"I was going to say, more private."

The way he said "private" made me more nervous. A bad kind of nervous.

"No, this is just fine with me."

I led him to a tall bar table lodged against the wall. Katie was four tables away, but within my line of sight.

Remember, Hope, it's just a date. And not even a real date. More like a fake date. And if anything bad happens . . . "homicidal maniac."

Clay grabbed a menu from between the salt and pepper shakers. "What do you suggest, the lobster thermidor or the foie gras?"

I stared at him blankly, unsure if he was serious.

He cracked a smile.

Whew. "I would suggest you look at the fried cheese balls."

"I hear it's a good year for fried cheese balls."

We both laughed. That broke the ice.

Clay set down his menu. "Actually, I think I'm going for something in the 'popper' category."

"Wise choice."

"So, Katie says you don't do this often."

"Eat?"

"Date."

My mouth went dry and I reached for something to

drink, but I didn't have anything. So I shot Katie a death glare. She just shrugged.

I turned back to Clay. "Katie's got a big mouth."

We settled on what we wanted, and I went to the bar to place our orders with Bess. I picked up two beers while I was at it, and made sure to hipcheck Katie on my way back.

"I didn't mean to get your friend in trouble," Clay said when I returned. "And really, I understand the whole not-dating thing. I . . . uh . . ." He looked down. "I remember Jimmy. He was a good kid. I was in college back when the accident happened, but I heard about it from my folks. I'm really sorry that happened to you."

I didn't know whether to go back and strangle Katie or to thank her for getting all that out of the way ahead of time. I certainly didn't want to have to cover that topic myself, and hearing him talk about it . . . it didn't hurt as much as I thought it would.

I guessed that was progress.

"Thank you," I finally said. "So, Mr. Clayton Thorndale, I peg you as a surfer."

He held up his hands, palms out. "Guilty as charged. Since we don't have a lot of oceans here in Idaho, what gave me away?"

"Your hair looks like it's right out of the Beach Boys."

"I'm not sure that's a compliment."

"Nothing wrong with the Beach Boys. I take it you don't spend a lot of time in Hopeless?"

"I come back a few times a year, and always for Mother's party. Otherwise, I live in Malibu."

"Sounds exotic."

"Malibu? The exotic part gets old fast. But surfing and the waves? Never."

"Ever been married?"

"Once. Ten years ago, for about ten minutes."

I raised an eyebrow. "Was she that bad?"

"Actually, *I* was that bad."

"A man taking responsibility? This I gotta hear."

"It's the truth. I was an idiot. She and I wouldn't have made it anyway, but I got us to the finish line more quickly."

I figured I'd steer us back into more comfortable territory. "So, Malibu. That's not cheap living. I guess being a Thorndale has its benefits."

"Oh, well, yes . . . but I haven't seen a dime of Mother's money since in a long time."

"I thought you had a trust fund."

His face reddened. "Technically, you're right. But I blew through that dough not long after I graduated."

"All of it?"

"I was young and very stupid."

"Then how do you afford Malibu?"

He smiled. "It's called a job."

I felt like an idiot. "But your mother . . . I remember her saying you were an incompetent lawyer."

"Wow, you do get right to it, don't you? To be honest, Mother's right. I never was a very good lawyer. That's not actually how I make my money. I own a surfboard company."

"Then why does your mom say you're a lawyer?"

"In her eyes, better to be an incompetent lawyer than a successful surf bum."

Bess brought out a variety of poppers and fried whatchamacallits and a pitcher of beer, and Clay and I kept talking. He told me about life as a surfboard executive in Malibu, and I told him all about being an investigative reporter in Portland. I had to admit, although my first impression of Clay had not been a very good one, he was a decent guy.

"So," he said, setting down his beer mug and pushing away the empty popper plate. "You're an investigative reporter, and yet not one mention of the elephant in the room."

"You talking about the dead butler elephant or the multimillion-dollar stolen painting elephant?"

"Both. I was anticipating at least a mild interrogation."

"What can I say? I can't interrogate while I'm eating. But now that my stomach's full of fried grease, Clayton Thorndale . . ."

"Used my full name. This can't be good."

"Did you kill Pimsey?"

"There we go. *Now* we're dating. Usually I don't get accused of murder until at least the second date. You move fast, Miss Walker."

I just stared at him, waiting.

"No," he said. "I didn't kill Pimsey." He took a big swig of his beer.

"And did you steal the Knutsen?"

"Now *that* . . . I sort of wish I had. But sadly, nope to that one as well."

"Who do you think did it?"

"It appears your sheriff thinks Mr. Snoot did it."

"I know what the sheriff thinks. What do *you* think?"

"I don't think it was Snoot. Speaking as an incompetent lawyer, he's an incompetent security man. As events have now proven. Art forgery? He doesn't have the brains. Or the balls. Speaking of which, I heard a story about you two."

"You mean how I kicked him in the family jewels?"

He laughed. "That's the one. Valerie told me. That's fantastic."

"So, if Mortimer Snoot didn't do it, who do you think did it?"

"I think it was a professional job."

"Okay, lay it out for me. How did it go down?"

He folded his hands and leaned over the table. "Okay. Somebody breaks into the house, picks the lock, then tries to replace the real painting with the fake. But Pimsey hears something, goes down to check, and catches the burglar in the act. The burglar bashes him on the head. Switches the painting. Takes Pimsey's key, locks up, and takes off. Easy peasy."

"There's just one problem," I said. "The Maglite. It's definitely Snoot's, and it's definitely the murder weapon. How did a burglar get hold of Snoot's flashlight?"

"I've already anticipated your question. It was Pimsey who took Snoot's flashlight. The burglar wrestled it away and used it to kill him. Like I said, easy peasy. Maybe I should be an investigative reporter. Or better yet, a sheriff."

"Stick to surfboards because how did Snoot's bloody flashlight end up inside his mattress?"

Clay took a sip of beer and thought about that. He shook his head. "Yeah, that's a good question. I've got nothing. But now you're confusing me. I got the impression you don't think Snoot did it, but now you're saying he did?"

"No, I don't think he did it. But I also don't think this was a burglar. This was an inside job, and whoever did it was trying to frame Snoot."

"Well, it's hard for me to believe that anyone in our household could have killed Pimsey. Or killed anyone, really."

"I can understand that. You know these people. But bear with me. For the moment, let's just say it *was* someone in the household. Who would be most likely?"

"I once again want to state my objection to this line of questioning . . ."

"Objection overruled."

He rolled his eyes and smiled. "Fine, Your Honor. For the sake of argument, the person in the household who would be most likely to kill someone . . . Well, that's easy. My mother."

"Wow. And you think *I'm* the one who gets right to the point."

He shrugged. "She's killed before."

"*What?*" I screeched.

Everyone in the bar looked over at us, and Katie stood up like she was coming to rescue me. But I waved her off.

I lowered my voice. "Your mother has killed before?"

Clay burst out laughing. "Well, I *assume* she has. You've met the woman, haven't you?"

"That wasn't funny."

"I gotta say, it sort of was. Seriously, though, I can't think of anybody more capable of something like that than Mother. But once again, I absolutely *don't* think she actually killed Pimsey. This is purely hypothetical."

"But she's hiding something," I said.

"What do you mean?"

"During our search for the painting, I happened upon a journal in her nightstand. She freaked out on me."

"Well, wouldn't you? It's a journal. It's probably private."

"I think there's more to it than that."

"You think she confessed to murdering her own butler—and stealing her own painting—in her journal?"

"I don't know. I just think I'd really like to see what's in it."

Clay smiled. He looked around the bar, then pressed his hands on the table and leaned in again.

"I could help you with that. But you'll have to trust me," he whispered.

"Trust you with what?"

"I get the idea that this really is more about the investigation for you than a real date."

"Is there a question in there somewhere?" I asked.

He tapped his fingers on the table and looked at me a little too intensely. "How about you meet me outside the mansion in two hours? Maybe you'll come because you actually like me. Or maybe you'll come strictly because of professional curiosity. But either way, I've got something to show you."

This was an odd turn. But he was right. I was curious.

"What?" I asked.

"That great house has a few secrets your search didn't uncover."

"What exactly are you talking about?"

Clay smiled. "I'm talking about a secret passageway." Then he stood. "And I'm giving you a chance to see it."

CHAPTER 20

You could argue that meeting up with a murder suspect late at night in a creepy location was not the most intelligent move on my part. It was also becoming a bit of a habit. Thankfully, being a good investigative reporter was not always about intelligence. Bulldogged determination was often the order of the day. And taking risks. And, as I approached the Thorndale estate that night, I very much hoped this was one risk I wasn't going to regret.

Clay Thorndale seemed like a nice enough guy. At least, that was my read on him back at the Library. He honestly didn't seem like the murdering kind. But that didn't mean I was feeling all that comfortable going into a secret passageway with him. Still, his mother was hiding something, and I wasn't going to miss the opportunity to find out what. I needed to see her journal.

I drove through the Thorndales' front gate—which stood wide open, the guardhouse empty—and parked. Clay Thorndale was waiting for me in the circular drive.

As soon as I climbed out of my car, I pointed back at the gate. "So, I know Snoot is the most incompetent security man in the world, but why have a gate if you're just going to leave it wide open? You don't even need a code or anything?"

Clay shrugged. "Nope."

"Are there security cameras?"

"Nope to that too."

"And the empty guardhouse?"

"Normally Snoot would be there, but he can't be on duty twenty-four hours. Listen, people like Pimsey, Scratchett, and Snoot? They've been at this house doing this job for many, many years. It's all they've ever known. I think old Snoot was afraid that if he put in fancy alarms and cameras . . ."

"He wouldn't be needed."

"Exactly. And where else would he go? What would he do?"

Clay led me around the house toward the back. It was a pleasant early fall evening, with just a hint of a chill. The night sky was mostly cloudless, allowing the stars and a small half-moon to light our way.

"So, Clay, gotta be honest. I may be a little rusty with this dating thing, but I take all those *Cosmo* surveys, and showing your date a secret passageway is high on the creepy scale."

He turned around. "You're here, aren't you?"

"I'm an investigative reporter. Like you said, I'm curious for a living. So, how secret is this passageway, anyway?"

"You mean, how many people know?"

"Yeah."

"I'm not exactly sure. Valerie and Kitty and I all know. But we swore each other to secrecy. As far as I know, none of us has ever told anyone."

We were in familiar territory now. I spotted the Thorndale pool up ahead, the infamous pool house tucked behind it. Both sat behind a black wrought-iron fence positioned just below the great house.

"Until now," I said.

He laughed. "When we were kids, it was a big secret. Now, it doesn't seem to matter as much."

"Anybody else know about it?"

"My father. He had the passageway built."

"Why?"

"Can't you guess?"

"I'd really rather not."

"Let's just say that my father liked to have his freedom from my mother."

"Ah. He strayed a little?"

"I'd say he probably strayed a lot."

"Did your mother know?"

"About the passageway, or the straying?"

"Both."

"She knew about the straying. I think a woman always knows those things. I also think it's some weird bargain that rich and powerful couples sometimes make."

"An inability to stay faithful to your vows is a precondition for being successful?" I asked.

"Something like that."

"That's pretty sad."

"Yeah. It is."

"Did your mother know about the passageway?"

"I honestly don't think so," Clay said.

"That's impossible. How could a woman live in a house for almost forty years and never know something like that?"

"Mother's not really the homemaker type. And it's not like she was looking for it."

"Then how'd you kids figure it out?"

"You're never going to believe it."

"Try me."

"We were playing hide-and-seek. There's a big walk-in closet attached to my parents' bathroom, and inside that closet was an old wooden wardrobe where my dad kept some of his suits. I went in there to hide, and my hand fell on a latch. I moved it, and something sprang open."

"You're kidding, right? You've just described the beginning of *The Lion, the Witch, and the Wardrobe.*"

"I said you wouldn't believe me. My dad apparently had a keen sense of adventure—and apparently he'd read the Narnia books. Anyway, I showed Kitty and Valerie, and of course we thought it was a wonder. I asked my dad about it, and he took me into his office and got very serious with me. He told me I must *never* tell my mother, or anybody else. This would be a secret between us kids and him."

"You didn't think that was weird?"

"Of course I did. But I didn't care. I mean, who gets a secret passageway in their house?"

"Why didn't you tell Sheriff Kramer about this?"

"I didn't want to be the one spilling my family's

secrets. And then Snoot got arrested, and it looked like maybe he did it."

"And now?"

Clay stopped and shrugged. "After talking to you, I'm not so sure."

We ducked behind a set of thick bushes that sat in front of the mansion like a leafy green wall. Clay pulled out his phone to use as a flashlight.

"Clay, if you're planning on killing me back here, I should warn you, I'm really good at kicking guys in their nether regions."

He laughed. But he didn't say anything. Which, if I'm being honest, made an already creepy situation suddenly seem much worse.

He stopped and knelt down. He was aiming his phone at the wall of the great house. I looked for a door, but there was none. Just a solid rock foundation.

Clay put his hand on one of the stones and pressed it. I heard a click, and to my surprise, a small section of the stone wall swung in, like a door on a hinge.

He motioned me forward. "Ladies first."

A man had been murdered in this great old house just a few days before. A multimillion-dollar painting had been stolen. And now a man I barely knew was inviting me to enter a dark hole in the wall.

Dumb risk or calculated risk—that was the question. Oh, who was I kidding? I was a sucker for a good story. And I loved tracking down clues. Earl had told me to go out and find some new evidence. This was my chance.

Still, I knew one thing for sure. I was *not* going in there first.

"I think I'll let you lead the way, okay?"

Clay crawled through the entrance on hands and knees. Like my granny, I was not a professional in the art of church and prayer. But I was smart enough to make the sign of the cross and ask God to cover my six, just in case.

I crawled through the opening. As soon as I was inside, the stone door closed behind me. It was dark as coal, and my heart began pounding away in my chest.

"Clay?" I said, not at all certain where he was.

His phone lit up. He was kneeling just a few feet away, smiling at me. "Sorry about that. Dropped my phone."

We were in a tiny crawlspace only a few feet square. On one side, a narrow wooden stairway angled upward sharply, like a ship's ladder, with railings on either side.

"Hope," Clay said, "you looked kind of freaked out. We don't really have to do this."

"You tell me that now? No, I've come this far. Show me this thing."

With his phone in one hand, Clay held the railing with the other, and I followed him up the stairs. As we climbed, I couldn't help but wonder why Valerie and Kitty hadn't told the sheriff about this secret. Maybe they didn't think it was relevant. Maybe they were still trying to keep their father's old secrets.

And maybe one of them had a secret of their own.

We reached a landing. The stairs continued up, but a dank and musty passageway stretched out before us.

Clay pointed his phone down the hall. "That way takes you to the main floor. Comes out just behind the grandfather clock."

"Of course it does. But we're not going that way?"

"No. You want to see the wardrobe."

We continued up. At the next landing, the stairs stopped. A narrow hallway led in two directions.

Clay pointed to our left. "This way to the wardrobe."

"What's the other way?"

"The observation deck."

"What the heck is that?"

"It's where my dad kept his telescope. In addition to being a serial philanderer, my father fancied himself an amateur astronomer. Plus, it made a great cover. On the rare occasion when Mother actually noticed he was gone, he would just say he was up with his telescope looking at the stars."

"Your father seems like kind of a bad dude."

"Maybe now it's easier to understand Mother."

I followed Clay down a very narrow hallway, my hands on his back. I felt like I was in high school and I was going through a haunted house with Jimmy. If Jimmy could see me now, I knew exactly what he would say. *"Hope, how can you possibly be this dumb?"*

At the end of the hall, Clay pointed his phone at the wall. There was a handle and the outline of a door.

"Is this the wardrobe?" I whispered.

He smiled. "Ready?"

I nodded.

Clay put a finger to his lips, then turned off his phone and took my hand. I heard a click and felt a rush of air. Clay pulled me forward.

This was definitely a wardrobe. We passed through clothes—smelly clothes. Probably Mr. Thorndale's old suits, hanging there since the day he died. Then we stepped through the clothes, and I could see.

We were in a large walk-in closet. A dim light shone through the open doorway ahead of us. Clay once again held his finger in front of his lips and motioned for me to follow.

We stepped out of a closet into a bathroom. The source of the glow was a night-light. It looked nothing like my *Hopeless News* vest. Not nearly yellow enough. We passed through the bathroom and into the bedroom of Isabelle Thorndale.

The old woman lay asleep, propped up with four or five large pillows. She was snoring loudly. On the nightstand was that same bottle of whiskey, along with assorted bottles of pills.

"Someone should tell your mother that whiskey and pills aren't really a good combination," I whispered.

"As long as that someone isn't me. Well . . ." He stepped aside. "Do your thing."

"Wait. You want me to go in there alone?"

"You're the one who wants to read the journal."

"No way. She's *your* mother. You go in there."

He grimaced. "Fine. We'll both go."

We tiptoed into her room. Part of me thought that a rhino could run through her room and she wouldn't hear it. The other part of me thought that a woman like Isabelle Thorndale might keep a sawed-off shotgun under her blankets, just waiting for some imbecile to try to steal her journal.

Clay grabbed the handle of the nightstand drawer and

started to pull. And right at that moment, the old woman's snoring stopped.

We both froze. For what seemed like an eternity, we just stood there. Sweat pooled below my armpits and started to drip down my sides. Was she awake? Had she heard us?

Then Isabelle started snoring again, and I relaxed.

Clay opened the drawer, took out the journal, and handed it to me. I slowly backed away from the bed, and Clay began to follow.

Again, the snoring stopped.

And I knew instantly, this time was different.

Isabelle screamed, and I ran. I ran through the bathroom, through the closet, through the wardrobe, and down the creepy dark hall. I was about to race down the stairs when I realized something that absolutely terrified me. Someone was coming *up* them. I couldn't see who it was—it was absolute pitch-black—but I *heard* them. I'm certain I peed my pants. I was trapped in a creepy dark hallway in an old mansion stuck between a screaming old lady and a mysterious figure. There was only one thing I could do.

I kept running.

Down the hall, toward the observation deck. Running blind. I smashed right into the wall, felt around, found a handle, and opened a door.

Finally, I could see again. I'd stepped out onto a second-story deck. Near the railing stood an old telescope. I ran to it and looked over. Below was the swimming pool I'd snuck into so many years ago, and behind it was the pool house I'd TP'd. But there was no way down from here. No way out.

I spun back around just in time to see a dark figure, dressed all in black, rush at me and hit me with both hands in my chest. I stumbled backward . . .

. . . And went over the railing.

CHAPTER 21

I figured I was dead. I struck the ground, and the wind rushed out of me. I turned instantly cold. But then I noticed why.

I was wet.

I hadn't hit the ground. I'd fallen into the pool.

For a moment I panicked, splashing about, trying to catch my breath. Then I found my way to the side of the pool and held on while I recovered my wits.

I looked up to the second-story deck. Perched just over the railing was that old telescope. But nothing and no one else. No dark figure. No Clay Thorndale.

It was then that I noticed the journal floating in the water next to me. I must have dropped it as I fell. It was soaked, but I grabbed it and pulled myself out of the water. I had to get out of there.

As I slipped through the wrought-iron fence, lights began turning on in the grand old house.

That was my cue.

I was wet and in serious pain, but I ran as fast as I

could to my car. I peeled out of the circular drive and sped my way through town, thankful that there was only one cop in Hopeless and he was too busy with a murder investigation to be setting up any speed traps. I parked in front of the Library, jumped out, let myself into the bar, and ran upstairs. I tore off my clothes, jumped into the shower, and let the hot water wash over me.

I tried very hard not to think about what had just happened.

When I got out of the shower, I threw on shorts and a T-shirt and went to see what state the journal was in. It was completely soaked. I mean completely. And unless I wanted all the pages and ink to stick and run together, I needed to dry it out.

I put the journal on the bathroom counter, then I put the hair dryer on the counter beside it, pointing at the journal. I turned it on, and let it run.

An enormous waste of electricity? Absolutely. Did I care? Not at all.

Just as I crawled under my covers, my phone buzzed. It was Clay. There was *no* chance I was answering that. I turned my ringer off and thanked God I was still alive.

And then, before I fell to sleep, I said what I had said every night for twelve straight years.

"Goodnight, Jimmy, wherever you are."

* * *

I DIDN'T DREAM about Jimmy and the accident that night. I dreamed of a scary dark figure. And falling to my death.

When I woke up, I found myself looking up at another

scary figure. But this one was not dark. She was pale, with skin as tough as leather and hair almost the color of snow. She wore a bright blue Boise State sweatshirt, and she was hovering over my head.

"Only ninety-seven hours left to paint the house."

I sat up.

Granny shook her head in disappointment. "You look like crap. You were out with that Thorndale boy."

"I *feel* like crap. But it's not even remotely what you think."

"What happened?"

"I honestly don't think you'd believe me."

"I once saw your grandfather eat sixty-two frog legs and then down an entire bottle of whiskey."

"That was actually you, Granny. You still have the ribbon hanging up in the bar."

She smiled. "That *was* me, wasn't it? You think I should get back into competitive eating?"

I rolled my legs over the side of the bed and stood up, my back absolutely killing me. "No, Granny, I don't."

"You don't think I've still got it?"

"The problem is, I'm *sure* you've still got it. It would be too easy for you to win."

Granny thought about that, then nodded in agreement. "Bar opens in an hour. In case you forgot how to tell time, that means you slept until eleven."

As she hobbled downstairs, I went to the bathroom. The hair dryer had turned off at some point during the night—it had tripped the GFI outlet. The pages were still a bit damp, though, so I reset the outlet and turned it back on.

I put on stretchy pants, a sports bra, a gray T-shirt, and a jean jacket. I even brushed my teeth. Then I walked over to my whiteboard. On one side, I'd written *Tommy Medola* at the top, and underneath that, *Mayor Wilma Jenkins* and *Yellow Palms LLC.* I wasn't done looking at the mayor and trying to figure out her connection to the Medola crime family, but right now, I had a different puzzle to solve.

I spun the whiteboard around to give myself a blank canvas.

I was lucky to have hit the water last night. Whoever pushed me over that railing couldn't have expected me to survive. Which meant somebody had tried to kill me. Somebody who knew about the Thorndales' secret passageway. And probably the same somebody who had killed Pimsey and stolen that Knutsen.

I was going to figure out who.

I wrote the names across the board. I started with the people who, according to Clay, definitely knew about the passageway.

Valerie Thorndale. Kitty Thorndale. Clay Thorndale.

Was Clay a suspect? He was the one who lured me to the passageway in the first place. But if he had wanted to hurt me, why not just do it in the passageway when he and I were all alone? Plus, there was no way he and the dark figure were the same person. He was behind me, probably trying to calm down his hysterical mother. Clay was a suspect only if he was working with somebody else. Was that possible?

Maybe.

But to be honest, I didn't think so. I didn't *like* like the guy, but I liked him. He was nice. Fun, even. I had to hand it to Katie—even though it sort of ended up being the worst date in human history, I had a good time before that. Clay wasn't someone I wanted to go on a second date with, but it had been nice to be out with a man again.

I crossed him off the list.

Who else might have known about the passageway? I wrote down the obvious name. *Isabelle Thorndale.*

Mrs. Thorndale certainly might have found out about the passageway at some point over the years. But she definitely wasn't the one who pushed me. I crossed her name off almost as soon as I'd written it down.

That left the help. I added five more names—Pimsey, Snoot, Scratchett, Schneider, and Juan. Pimsey was dead. I crossed him off. And Juan? It just seemed too improbable to me. Why would he go out of his way to make a connection with me? Why would he want help figuring out what his niece was up to if he knew that I might also be investigating a crime he was involved in? Plus, he had never lived at the mansion and wouldn't have been there the night of Pimsey's death. Of all the help, he was the least likely to know about a secret passageway. I crossed off Juan, too.

And then there was Snoot. He certainly could have known about the passageway, but he had the perfect alibi for last night—he was in jail. So I crossed him off too.

There was one more name to consider. Mr. Sokolov. He seemed the least likely to know about the secret passageway, and plus, he was such a tiny and delicate man. The figure who attacked me had strength. Nope. Sokolov was not my dark figure. I wrote his name down anyway just so I could cross it off.

That left four names on my whiteboard. Valerie Thorndale, Kitty Thorndale, Mrs. Scratchett, and Mrs. Schneider. Four women. Could any of them have been the figure who pushed me? All were strong women. Mrs. Schneider worked with her hands and certainly looked strong. Mrs. Scratchett was wiry, but feisty. I was willing to bet she'd been in a few fights in her day. Kitty Thorndale was a piece of work—she'd be more than capable of handling herself in any situation. And Valerie? At first glance, she didn't seem the fighting type. But there was something about her. A strength. A simmering, deep down below. Maybe she was the type of woman willing to do whatever it took.

So. Four suspects. All women. One of them was a killer.

Hopefully, the journal would help me figure out who.

The next thing I did was check my phone. I had several calls and texts from Clay. He could wait. I also had a series of texts from Katie.

How was the hot date?

That bad? Or that good? Can't tell what the silence means.

Okay, if you're trapped in the trunk of a car, kick out the taillight and leave some kind of trail. I have a particular set of skills that makes me good at finding people like you.

Okay, nerd, stop ducking my messages. Taking kids to a doctor appointment now. Call me later.

Unless you're still in the trunk of a car. Then get a weapon, anything, and go for his face as soon as he opens the trunk.

It was nice that Katie was covering all the bases.

Finally I checked on the journal. It was just about dry.

It was time to see what secrets Isabelle Thorndale was hiding.

* * *

"I've been coming here for three weeks now. What do you know about me?" I asked Nick, the hipster millennial who manned the counter at A Hopeless Cup.

I had decided that as much as I wanted to read that journal, a woman who has just almost fallen to her death deserves a good cup of coffee before she does anything else.

Nick handed me my grande white mocha and rang me up. "You mean, other than you like white mochas and you're old?"

"Do you think being a barista gives you some sort of diplomatic immunity that allows you to call me old?"

"I think the only people who use phrases like 'diplomatic immunity' are old people."

"If it wasn't for the fact that you made me a beautiful cup of coffee, I would rip off your man bun and shove it up your French press."

"You sound angry. Don't worry, I'm sure it's just hormones. My mom's going through menopause too." Nick smiled. "See you tomorrow, ma'am."

"Menopause? Why, you—"

"Are you going to punch him, Hope?"

The voice behind me gave me that fingernails-on-chalkboard feeling. The noxious perfume smell that came along with it made me feel like I might dry heave.

I turned around to see Gemima Clark, my enemy since birth.

My relationship with Nick was simple. I hated him—I loved his coffee. My relationship with Gemima was also simple. I hated her—I loved nothing about her. If only all relationships could be so easy.

"He called me old," I said. "He always calls me old."

She looked at me like I was an overflowing trash receptacle. "You *are* old, Hope."

"We're the same age, Gemima."

"That might be true. But only one of us *looks* old, and it might be the one of us who thinks haute couture begins and ends with stretchy pants."

"Hey! On behalf of all women, lay off the stretchy pants. Stretchy pants are a sort of miracle that takes all your weird spots and puts them in the right spots."

She shook her head and patted me condescendingly on the shoulder. "You sad little creature. You really believe that, don't you?"

"I'll answer that if you answer this. What are you doing joining forces with a snake like Mayor Jenkins?"

"You're truly pathetic, Hope. Wilma is the most ambitious and successful woman in the region. Something you should aspire to instead of trying to drag down."

"Yes, Wilma is ambitious. I'll give you that. But so is the mob. And—funny thing—she's *involved* with the mob."

Gemima rolled her eyes. "Not this again."

"Yes, Gemima, this again. Just listen. Do I hate your guts? Of course I do. Does the sight of your face make me throw up a little in my mouth? Absolutely. But you and I go back a long way. I sort of was hoping you and I could hate each other the rest of our lives."

"What are you talking about?"

"Wilma Jenkins is tied up with some really, really bad people. Just be careful what you're getting into."

"You know what, Hope? I'm going to love it when Wilma takes a bulldozer to that stupid cabin and turns your favorite spot in the world into a concrete parking lot." Gemima winked. "And for the record, those stretchy pants don't quite put *everything* where it should be." She cocked her head and looked at my rump. Then she strutted her perfect little self out of there.

"You forgot to order a coffee!" I shouted after her.

CHAPTER 22

I sat down at a corner table, sure to point my butt as far away as possible from the good people of Hopeless, Idaho. I took a long, satisfying sip of my grande white mocha. I was about to dive into Isabelle's journal when my phone buzzed. I expected to see another call from Clay. Instead, it was a call from my newest contact.

"Hello?"

"Hi, Hope. It's Bev up at the high school. I've got some information for you about Carlos."

"Wow, that's great! How'd you do that?"

"Well, I got to thinking. If I was as worried about someone as it appears Juan is, I'd like to know as much as possible. So when April went to the restroom earlier and left her phone behind . . ."

"You didn't."

"I'm a little ashamed of myself, but yes, I looked up his contact info. I have a number for you."

"You did the right thing."

"I'm not sure if I did, but like I said, I just want to make sure she's okay. Can you keep my involvement secret?"

"You can count on it."

I wrote down the number on a scrap of paper, then dialed up an old friend. His full name was Charles Dewickey, but I'd only ever heard him answer to his nickname, Darwin. Darwin was the IT guy at my old paper, the *Portland News Gazette*. He was wicked smart, and a crack researcher who'd been able to help me out from time to time.

"Hope?"

"Darwin, my love."

"I talked to my mom about you, Hope."

"I trust it was all good."

"She says you're probably not really my girlfriend."

"Your mom is a wise woman."

"So, you admit it?"

"I do, Darwin. I am not your girlfriend. I'm something much, much better."

"There's something better than a girlfriend?"

"Are you kidding me? Darwin, don't you feel what I feel?"

"I'm not sure. What do you feel?"

"Darwin, you and me? We're like Sonny and Cher."

"Never heard of them."

"Okay, we're like peanut butter and jelly."

"We're condiments?"

"Are peanut butter and jelly condiments? I thought they were spreads."

"What's the difference?"

"Well, one is . . . okay, I don't really know. Besides,

we're getting off topic. The point is, you and I are soul mates. Soul mates, I tell you."

Darwin didn't sound satisfied. "Is that really better than boyfriend and girlfriend?"

"Darwin, I feel like you don't get out enough. I'll tell you what I'm going to do. I'm going to take a selfie right now, and then I'm going to send it to you with a filter that makes my face look like a pig's face."

"Why would you do that?"

"Because, Darwin—soul mates."

"I am so confused."

"Don't be. Just know this. The love between soul mates is a love that can never die. Now that we've gotten that out of the way, have you learned anything more about Mayor Wilma Jenkins?"

"Um, yeah, sort of. Nothing more about the business workings of Yellow Palms, or anything related to it . . ."

"But?"

"Mayor Jenkins took a trip."

"Lots of people take trips, Darwin."

"She took a trip to Aruba on February eighteenth of this year."

"And why is this news?"

"Apparently, she went on the trip to learn more about the tourism industry."

"Well, Wilma does want to make Hopeless a great tourist destination. You know, for a couple of soul mates, I'm not sure we're on the same wavelength."

"Or maybe I just like making you wait for the good stuff. Someone else was also in Aruba on February eighteenth."

"Oooh, the plot thickens. Who? Don't tell me Tommy Medola's wife was there at the same time."

"Much, much better. Tommy Medola *himself* was there."

"Shut up! You're sure?"

"Check this out."

My phone buzzed with a text from Darwin. It contained a photo of a newspaper clipping. Local officials and visiting businessmen were posing for the camera, and second from the left was none other than Tommy Medola.

"Darwin, what are the chances that this was a total coincidence?"

"I'd say not very good."

Another text came in. Another photo. I opened it up. It was a paparazzi photo of the actor Nate Pittman and his newest flame.

"Darwin, why am I looking at a picture of Nate Pittman?"

"Look who's sitting behind him."

I zoomed in on the picture. It was none other than Tommy Medola. He was having dinner with a woman, but I couldn't see who the woman was. Her face was obscured behind her brown hair.

"I see Tommy Medola eating dinner, but . . . so what?"

"It's fun to make you squirm, Hope. Check out the hand."

The hand? Tommy and the woman were holding hands, but . . . "I'm not seeing what you want me to see, Darwin."

"The woman's hand, Hope! You know, for a couple of

soul mates, I'm pretty sure I'm the peanut butter and you're the jelly."

"I like the jelly."

"So do I."

"Darwin, just tell me about this picture."

"Look closely at that woman's hand. It's got a fancy diamond ring on it and a matching diamond bracelet around her wrist. I've looked at countless photos of Mayor Jenkins, and she's always wearing a big diamond ring and a fancy bracelet. So I blew the picture up and compared it. Hope, I'm pretty sure the woman in that photo is Wilma Jenkins."

"Darwin, you're amazing."

"I know."

"And do you know what this means?"

"No. What does it mean?"

"We're not soul mates."

"We're not?"

"No, Darwin. We're better than soul mates. We're *super* soul mates."

"That sounds like something you just now made up."

"Oh, Darwin, you kid. Hey, I've got one more thing—and this one's simple. I've got a number. The name attached to the number is Carlos. I need everything you can find on this guy. How long will that take?"

"It depends."

"On what?"

"On whether you made up super soul mates just now."

"Thanks, Darwin. Let me know what you find."

"Bye, Hope."

After the call, I finally turned my attention to the journal. It was, as I'd assumed, a personal diary. I started at the back—at the present day—and worked my way backward. If Isabelle Thorndale was hiding something related to Pimsey's murder or the theft of her painting, the recent entries would be where I was most likely to find it.

You know what they say about how people from the old days had such beautiful handwriting? That didn't apply to Isabelle Thorndale. Her writing was somewhere on the spectrum between busy emergency room doctor and maniacal conspiracy theorist. But as I worked backward, the handwriting gradually became easier to read, and the content was in many ways more meaningful. Her most recent entries often seemed impatient and hurried, but earlier in her life, she seemed to take her time. I couldn't believe how many years she'd squeezed into this one lousy book. I soon realized that was because she didn't journal often. Most years had only a few entries. For 1982, she only had one entry. It said *SUCKED BIG TIME EXCEPT FOR REAGAN!*

I felt somebody hovering over me. I snapped the book shut and looked up—right into the perfect green eyes of none other than Alex Kramer.

My heart pounded in my chest. Then I regrouped.

"Why, hello, Sheriff."

He looked down at me and smiled. I wondered if he knew the power he had when he smiled at a woman.

"Hello, Hope." He nodded at my cup. "What's your poison?"

"White mocha."

"Sounds good to me."

He turned and walked to the front counter. I thought

about sticking around, but then I remembered the journal. The one that I'd stolen. The one that was currently in my hands.

"Nice seeing you, Sheriff," I said. I stood up and began toward the door.

He held up a finger. "Hold up. I actually wanted to talk with you. Can you stay around for a minute and chat?"

Shoot, I thought as I sat back down and slipped the journal under the table. "I guess I have a minute."

Alex picked up a grande white mocha, then joined me at my table. He took a long sip and smiled.

"Are you mad at me?" he asked.

"Why would I be mad?"

"On account of me trying to keep you out of my investigation."

"Me? Mad? Whatever gave you that idea?"

"It's just the way you're tensing your jaw. And then there's the complete absence of a smile. It seems like you might be mad."

I leaned forward. "Listen . . . Alex, is it?"

"You know it's Alex."

"So the thing is, I didn't give it much thought."

"You didn't? Oh, good, because I thought—"

I slammed my hand on the table. "You escorted me away from the crime scene two times. That's twice, in case you're not up to speed. I don't see you doing that to anybody else around here."

"Listen, Hope. You must understand why I can't have you investigating crimes. First off, it's dangerous. Second, it's not your job."

"Have you forgotten that I just solved two murders?"

"You've only reminded me of it five hundred times."

"And currently, I am a gainfully employed reporter for the *Hopeless News*. Which means, in addition to me being a great investigator, it *is* my job to investigate whatever is newsworthy in the lovely town of Hopeless, Idaho. And in case you didn't know, a murder and a multimillion-dollar art heist qualify as 'newsworthy.'"

"But Hope . . . and I hate to bring this up again. . . you *did* get fired from your last job as an investigator."

Oh, no, he didn't.

"Now you're just trying to piss me off. Listen, Sheriff. Have you ever thought about *why* I was fired the very same day my explosive investigative story on the Medola crime family was about to run? Do you think it was because I was such a bad investigator that Tommy Medola got hold of the story, read it, and said to himself, 'Wow, she's no good. I've done all sorts of illegal stuff she never found. We need to get her fired and find someone more competent so they can send me to jail for the rest of my life!'"

"I'm starting to see your point."

"I hope so. Tommy Medola got me fired because I *did* find the truth—and because that truth was going to jeopardize everything for him. I got *fired* because I am one *hell* of a good investigator."

Alex held up his hands in surrender. "I give up. Mea culpa. But Hope, as sheriff of this town, investigating crime is *my* job."

I shrugged. "As the newspaper reporter in this town, maybe it's my job too."

I could see Alex was not convinced.

I leaned forward. "Hear me out. For whatever reason, our entire town pays for only one official law enforcement officer—you. Plus one part-time secretary—Katie. That's it. And that's ridiculous for the size of our town. You're understaffed. So as long as I work for an entity whose job it is to find the truth, why not let me investigate? You know you could use the extra manpower."

He looked uneasy. "It's . . . highly unorthodox."

"It wouldn't be official. And here's the important part —you wouldn't get in my way anymore."

He shook his head. "I just don't think I can agree, Hope."

"You're threatened by me, aren't you?"

"What?"

"That's it, isn't it? Strong, capable woman. This is sexism, plain and simple."

"Now you're out of line."

"Or is it simpler than that? Ah . . . it is, isn't it? You're not threatened because I'm a *woman*. You're threatened because I'm *a better investigator*. You're scared, Alex Kramer."

He sat up straighter. "I'm not scared. Not of you."

"Then prove it. I say we make a wager. Whoever solves this case first, wins."

"You're out of your mind."

"And you're out of excuses."

"Okay, fine. You're on. Whoever solves the case first, wins."

"Great. If I win, you stay out of my way and let me investigate crimes—"

"Fine, and if *I* win—"

I held up a hand. "Tut tut! Manners! I wasn't done. You let me investigate crimes *and...*"

"There's an *and?*"

"Yes, there's an and. *And* you spend an entire Saturday helping me paint my grandmother's house."

"That's ridiculous. I would never agree to that."

"Why not? You'd only have to do it if you lost the bet. Are you afraid you'll lose the bet? Because I'm the better investigator? Is that what you're saying?"

"Fine! And if I win—no, *when* I win—you will *stop* investigating crimes. Permanently. You will stay in your own lane. You will report about new births, stray kittens, and the occasional thieving fox. *And* . . . you will spend an entire Saturday helping me clean out my new apartment. It's a complete mess. Unless, that is, you think you're going to lose."

I shot my hand out. "We have a deal, Sheriff Krompel."

"It's Kramer," he growled.

"I've heard it both ways."

He took my hand and squeezed it. "I'm not kidding here. If you lose, you stop getting in my way once and for all and let me do my job."

"Fine."

He stood up. "Then we've got a deal. Now if you'll excuse me, I need to visit the little boys' room. Good luck, Hope." He smirked. "You'll need it."

I hated when Alex smirked. And I hated it even more when he smirked while wearing those dorky sheriff's clothes.

I needed to win this bet. *Bad.*

While Alex was in the bathroom, I quickly dove back

into Isabelle Thorndale's journal. This time, I opened it up to a random page near the beginning. And as luck would have it, I found something good.

Really good.

It seemed that Mr. Thorndale wasn't the only one who had strayed. Isabelle Thorndale was unfaithful as well. And for *her* extramarital affair, sneaking out of the house wasn't even necessary.

Oh, my.

I jumped up to leave—then noticed that Alex had left his phone on the table.

Along with his car keys.

The thing was, a bet was a bet. And a head start wouldn't be such a bad thing.

I really didn't like to lose.

I grabbed Alex's keys and hustled out of A Hopeless Cup. I didn't want to keep his keys—just . . . slow him down a bit. So I found his truck and threw his keys in the back. If he asked me, I could tell him I put them someplace safe.

Did I feel a little bad about what I was doing? Yes. But only a little. Very, very little.

I ran to my car, started it up, and peeled out. You see, I had figured out what Isabelle Thorndale had been trying to hide.

Once upon a time, Isabelle Thorndale and Walter Pimsey were in love.

CHAPTER 23

I was sitting in my car outside Katie's house, trying to piece it all together, when the text came in.

Hope, it's Alex. Did you see my keys when you were at the coffee shop?

Hmmm. To lie or not to lie—that was the question. It seemed a tad ironic to begin a search for truth with a lie. So I decided for ignorant noncommitment.

Pretty sure you had them. Why?

Can't find them. Looked everywhere.

Have you tried Albania?

Albania? No. What are you talking about?

Then you haven't looked everywhere. Sorry, gotta run.

I turned off the phone and laughed. Alex Kramer was going to be mad. But what could I do? The guy had a bad habit of leaving his keys in his truck.

I knocked on Katie's front door, and a small creature opened it. The creature was wearing shoulder pads, Incredible Hulk slippers, and a Freddie Kruger mask.

"Looking good, Dominic!"

"Thanks, Aunt Hope!"

"Your mom like you answering the door looking like the scariest creature in the world?"

"She likes when I scare away the salesmen and the Baptists."

"Does it work?"

"Once I start screaming, they almost always leave. One time I had to kick the vacuum cleaner guy in the shins."

"Your mom is lucky to have you."

"That's what I keep telling her."

I found Katie folding laundry in the living room. Lucy was doing some weird dance in the corner. Celia was throwing Cheerios.

"What's up, Katie?"

"You know, living the dream."

"What exactly is Lucy doing?"

"Elmo had a stupid segment on mimes yesterday. So now I get a full day of Lucy pretending she's Marcel Marceau. It's weird, but . . . it's quiet. I'll take it."

"Looks like Celia is redecorating."

"Cheerio is the new beige. It goes with everything."

"I need some help."

Katie threw a stack of underwear on the table. "I don't need to buy beer for you anymore. Trust me, you look old enough."

"The barista at the coffee shop thinks I'm really old."

"That idiot Nick? Chris had to hold me back from punching him last week."

"Why? What'd he do?"

"He asked me whether I was having a boy or a girl."

"Don't worry, Katie. Someday Nick the Idiot Millennial Man Bun Barista will have a mortgage and back fat and he won't be able to remember his own children's names. It happens to everyone."

"I really hope I'm alive to see that," Katie said wistfully. "And rip the man bun right off his stupid head. So, what do you need help with?"

"I found out some new information in the Thorndale case, but I still can't put it all together. So I need you to commit a crime."

"You came to the right place. Can the kids help?"

"I was sort of counting on it."

* * *

KATIE and I gave the children instructions, then we set up for our demonstration. To represent the Knutsen, Lucy had drawn a picture of a man on a horse. It was surprisingly good. We'd set it on a chair in the middle of the living room.

"How again is this supposed to help?" Katie asked.

"I don't know—give us a fresh perspective. Help us get inside the mind of a killer."

"If you say so." Katie turned and yelled, "Kids! Make Mama proud!"

Dominic came into the living room looking like a cartoon supervillain. He was holding the "fake Knutsen." Dominic had drawn this one himself. It was surprisingly bad. It looked less like "guy on horse" and more like "watermelon balanced on triangle." Dominic tiptoed over to the chair, took the "real Knutsen," and replaced it with the fake.

Then Lucy walked in. "Hark! Who goes there?" she yelled.

Dominic wasted no time. He grabbed the plunger and whacked Lucy across the head. She stumbled back and forth in a fashion so dramatic that William Shatner would be proud. Finally, she fell to the floor and let out a really horrible gurgling sound until her eyes closed and she was done.

Dominic grabbed a key from her and left the living room, pretending to lock an invisible door on his way out.

Katie broke into applause. "Bravo! Bravo, children!"

"Okay," I said. "What did we learn?"

Katie scratched her chin. "Lucy's super good at dying."

"You know, she really is."

Lucy blushed as if this was the highest compliment a person could receive.

Dominic came back in. "Did I do a good job whacking her, Mom?"

"Excellent, Dominic. You've got the makings of a really fine killer someday."

"I'm not sure you're allowed to say that," I said.

"We have very low expectations around here, Hope. That way, it's easy for the kiddos overachieve!"

"Okay, but this little play made me think of one thing. If Dominic needed Lucy's key to lock up, how did he get through the locked door to enter in the first place?"

"Dominic," Katie said, "do you have a good answer for Aunt Hope?"

"I can walk through walls."

"See, Hope?" Katie said. "It's so simple. Bet you didn't think of that."

"I'm beginning to understand your whole thing about low expectations."

"Atta girl. Now, Dominic," Katie said, "this time, try picking the lock on your way in."

Katie yelled action, and the kids went through the crime again. And again, and again. We did some where the murderer entered the room first, some where the butler entered first. And each time, Lucy's death scene was more dramatic than the last. In fact, it was getting rather disturbing. Way too many slurps and gurgles for my taste.

"Anything jump out at anybody?" Katie asked.

"Other than Pimsey takes forever to finish dying?" I said. "Well, I am curious about the scenario where Pimsey is in the room first. That does seem to be the most likely, since he has the only key, but . . . why? What would he be doing there?"

"Maybe he decided to check on the painting before the big reveal," Katie suggested.

"And the murderer art thief just happens to be nearby, waiting with the fake painting just in case?"

"You got any better ideas?"

I thought about it. Could the thief have picked the lock, and Pimsey caught them? It was possible. But *if* Pimsey was in the room first, why would that be?

"There's really only one reason why Pimsey would enter the room first," I said.

"What's that?"

"What if Pimsey was the one trying to steal the painting?"

Katie nodded thoughtfully. "Okay . . . okay, let's run with that. Someone catches him, kills him . . ."

"And then they see an opportunity to steal the painting and become very, very rich."

"I don't know . . ." Katie didn't look convinced.

I wasn't real happy with the theory either.

Katie was looking at the two drawings Lucy and Dominic had done. It had been easy to decide which one we would use as the "fake." Dominic's. The drawing I now thought of as *Watermelon on Triangle*. But as Katie studied them, she snapped her fingers. "You said the fake Knutsen was an expert forgery, right?"

"Yes. Unlike Dominic's."

"Meh. He always has murder to fall back on. His whacking was exquisite."

"So, what are you getting at?" I asked.

"You've been focused on the murder. Maybe you should look in a different direction."

"The painting!" I said.

Katie smiled. "Exactly. Someone forged that painting. Maybe you can figure out who. And that will lead you to the killer."

Katie was right. I needed to take this investigation in a new direction. I needed to focus on the painting itself. The problem was, I knew nothing about art. I needed an art expert.

My first thought was to call Bev at the high school. But then I remembered she said that Juan's niece was probably the most gifted artist she'd ever had. Maybe I could kill two birds with one stone. I'd promised Juan I'd check up on his niece, and hopefully she could tell me something about this painting.

It was time I talked to April.

CHAPTER 24

When I walked into the hardware store, Stank had a lawnmower flipped over and was busy sharpening a blade. When he saw me, he lifted his glasses off his nose and hung them around his neck.

"Oh, please tell me you wrote something really nasty about Gemima on the water tower," he said with a smile.

"Not yet, Stank. But give it time—the day is still young."

"That's the spirit. Need another water bottle? A mosquito tent? Testosterone treatment?"

"Testosterone treatment?"

"Hey, it's good for cash flow."

"Actually, I need to speak to your employee . . . April."

"I wish you could."

"She busy?"

"She's not here."

"I texted Juan—he said she was at work."

"And I was just about to call Juan as soon as I got Mr.

Bentley's mower ready. Which, by the way, April was supposed to have done for me. That girl can fix anything. But she never showed up."

"Does she do that very much?"

"Not show up? April might be moody, but she's always on time. I figured whatever it is, it must be important."

I immediately called Bev.

"Hi, Hope. What's up?"

"Any chance April is there working on an art project?"

"No. Why?"

"I came to Stank's to ask her a question about painting, but she didn't show up for work. Stank says that's not like her. You think she might be with Carlos?"

"I don't know. But she did step out in the hall on her cell phone today. Could have been talking to him."

"Please call me if you hear from her."

"I will."

I took out the piece of paper where I'd written down Carlos's number. But I hesitated.

I called Darwin instead.

"Hi, Hope."

"Hello, my dear."

"I prefer Darwin."

"How about Snuggle Bunny?"

"Darwin's good."

"Any chance you found out anything about that number?"

"Yep. It's a burner phone. Not registered to anyone."

"Crap."

"I wasn't finished. It's a burner phone. Not registered

to anyone. But it's still a phone, and that means, if you know a guy, you also know how to trace the phone."

"Darwin, you brilliant man."

"'Brilliant man' is much better than 'Snuggle Bunny.' I'll text you the address now."

I'd been on every street in Hopeless at some point in the first nineteen years of my life, but I didn't recognize this address. I punched it into my mapping app and followed the directions. It took me two miles outside of Hopeless, then onto a gravel road deep into the forest. After another half mile, the app said I'd arrived at my destination.

Apparently, my destination was a small gray house set way back from the road. A rusted-out pickup and an old Ford sedan were parked in a dirt driveway.

I had a bad feeling about this.

I walked up the steps and knocked on the door.

The man who answered looked to be in his early fifties. His hair was dark brown with flecks of gray, and his skin light brown. Probably Hispanic. He wore old jeans, work boots, and a blue flannel shirt. His jaw was tight and his eyes were fierce.

"Can I help you?" he asked.

"Is your son here?"

"My son? What are you talking about?"

"I was wondering if your son Carlos was here."

"Is this some kind of joke? I don't have a son named Carlos." He stepped forward, close to me, and stared right down at me. "I *am* Carlos."

My heart began pounding in my chest. April had a boy.

A boy named Carlos. The problem was, that boy wasn't a boy. He was a man.

A very scary man.

I turned around, my keys clutched in my hand. I looked at my car. I could try to make a run for it. I could call Alex. Or I could do something else.

I decided on something else.

I spun around, kicked Carlos in the shins, then rushed past him into the house, screaming April's name.

Ahead of me, a figure popped in through the open back door. Blue jeans. Bomber jacket. Frizzy black hair. April. Her face was full of shock and confusion.

I grabbed her hand. "We're getting out of here—now!"

I started pulling her out of the house, but she ripped her hand away from mine. Carlos came in the front door, holding his leg, his face full of rage.

I pulled out my phone. "Fine, I'm calling the police."

April and Carlos looked at each other, then as one, they shouted, "No!"

"What do you think is going on here?" Carlos asked.

"It's pretty obvious. A grown man and a teenage girl. You should be ashamed."

"What?" April said. "Y-you think . . .?" She shuddered. "Oh, gross. No! Carlos isn't . . . It's not like that. You've got it all wrong. You don't understand."

"What don't I understand?"

"Carlos isn't some creepy old dude. Carlos . . . he's my dad."

* * *

CARLOS MADE me a cup of coffee while I sat down and did my best to explain what I was doing there.

"Your Uncle Juan knows that I'm an investigative reporter. He asked for a favor. He said that at the end of last school year, you started to change. He's been concerned. He asked me to look into it."

"He wanted you to spy on me?"

"No. He just wanted to make sure you weren't in trouble. That's all. Your uncle loves you, April. He was worried that if he looked into it, you'd react exactly the way you're reacting right now. April, what's going on? Juan said you hadn't seen your dad since you were little."

"She hadn't," Carlos said. "And I'll keep that shame with me the rest of my life."

"But then, a few months ago, he showed up," April said.

"Just like that? After all these years?"

"I left her," Carlos said. "That's on me. I was immature. And I got into trouble. I was on the run. And then . . . then I didn't know where she was."

"When he reappeared, I was angry with him, at first," April said. "But then after he explained, I forgave him." She smiled up at Carlos.

"Why didn't you tell your uncle about this?" I asked. "He's been worried sick."

"Juan never liked me much," Carlos said. "Plus, my immigration status is, to put it mildly, in question. We were worried what might happen if Juan found out."

Carlos went on to explain that he had been working odd jobs while studying to get his GED. April had helped him find this small house to rent—paid in cash. And she'd been meeting him regularly to help him get ready for the GED.

"Wow," I said. "I really jumped to the wrong conclusions. I'm sorry."

"It's okay," April said. "You were just trying to help my uncle. I guess I should thank you . . . for caring to come find me today. You don't even know me."

I took another sip of coffee. "To be honest, it wasn't completely selfless."

"How do you mean?"

"I had another reason for looking for you at Stank's."

April looked suspicious. "Which was . . .?"

"Mrs. Hamilton said you're the best student she's ever had."

"She said that?"

"Yep. She showed me some of your work. It was amazing. Seems like you can do just about any style. So when the story I'm working on involved a painting, and I needed an art expert, I thought of you."

"Wow! Okay, cool. What do you want to know?"

"How hard is it to copy a painting perfectly? For a good painter."

"For a good painter? Not that hard. What's hard is the little stuff. Since you don't get to watch that other person paint, it's hard to know exactly how hard they pressed, what exact brush they used, stuff like that. Why do you ask?"

I shook my head. "It's probably a shot in the dark, but . . ." I took out my phone and pulled up a picture of the Knutsen. "How hard do you think it would be to paint something like this?"

I turned the phone around and showed her.

As soon as April saw the photo, she gasped. Then she covered her mouth and looked over at her dad. He snatched the phone out of my hand and looked at it. Then he reached over the table, grabbed me by my shirt collar, and held tight.

"What are you *really* doing here?" he growled.

"Let go of me," I said, trying to release myself from his iron grip.

"Why did you come?"

And that's when it hit me.

I knew who the forger was. It was the best student Bev Hamilton had ever had. The girl who could paint practically anything.

Even a ten-million-dollar painting.

"It was you," I said, looking at April.

Carlos held me even tighter. The look on his face was the same look any parent would have when they're trying to protect their child from harm.

But all of a sudden, April ran into him like a linebacker and pushed him away from me. I got my shirt and my breath back. I should have run out of there right that second and called Alex. But I didn't.

I'd been a teenage girl. I'd had a parent run out on me when I was young. And as I looked at this girl, I knew I wasn't looking at the face of a hardened criminal. This was a scared kid.

Something I understood all too well.

I reached my hand out to April, and she reluctantly grabbed it. Then she burst into tears.

I pulled her in close and held her for a long, long while.

When she'd gotten most of it out of her system, she let go of me, wiped away the tears, and looked me in the eye, as if judging whether or not this total stranger could be trusted. Then she drew a deep breath.

"Yes," she said. "It was me."

CHAPTER 25

Carlos apologized for putting his hands on me. Said he went temporarily insane. I told him I understood. Plus, I *had* kicked him in the shins. And if he'd held me much longer, I'd have kicked him someplace else. That made him smile.

He poured me another cup of coffee, and this time we walked out the back door to a small brick patio that had been transformed into something else.

"A studio?"

April nodded. "It's a nice place to paint."

One of those paintings was sitting on an easel. It was a landscape, showing a family fishing along the Moose River. It was only half finished, but like the rest of her paintings I'd seen, it was very good.

"It's beautiful," I said.

"Thank you."

"So," I said. "How . . .?"

"First, I had no idea the painting would be used in a crime. You have to believe me. As soon as Uncle Juan told me about what happened to the butler, I had a very bad feeling. And then when he told me the real painting had been stolen, then I knew what I'd been part of. I wanted to tell Uncle Juan. Or the sheriff. But I thought they'd throw me in jail. Or at the very least, I thought my dad would get in trouble."

"Who hired you to paint the fake?"

"I have no idea."

"How is that possible?"

"It was all handled online. I have an account at this big freelance artist site called Multilancer.net. I got a message two months ago asking me if I'd ever seen the Thorndales' Knutsen. I said of course. They sent me a high-resolution photo of the painting, along with its dimensions, and asked me to paint an exact replica. They didn't call it a forgery."

"But deep down, you knew, didn't you?"

"At first, I told myself someone just wanted a copy of the painting. But yeah, there was a part of me that wondered what it was being used for. And I did it anyway. Because the money was good."

"How much?"

"Five hundred dollars put into my Paypal account when I took the job. Another five hundred dollars upon completion. I was trying to help my dad get set up out here in his own place. Just enough cash until he earned a few paychecks of his own. I thought the money was an answer to my prayers."

"Did you ship it somewhere? Deliver it?"

"That part freaked me out the most. I had my dad with me just in case. I was instructed to wrap it in brown paper, then set it behind the rest stop five miles out of town. That's when I couldn't fool myself anymore. I knew something bad was going on. And now I feel like it's my fault that poor man is dead."

"You can't do that to yourself, April. We still don't know what happened. And maybe there's a way for us to keep your involvement a secret while I find out the truth. Would you be willing to help me with that?"

She looked at her dad. He nodded.

She looked me in the eye. "Yes, I'd like that very much."

"Do you still have all your communications about the painting?"

She grabbed her backpack and pulled out a laptop. She went to her Multilancer site and pulled up her communications. The buyer had the user name FALCON4848. I ran through the messages, then dialed Darwin.

"I didn't know having a girlfriend would be so much work," he said when he answered.

"But when you and I finally go out on our big date, you'd better believe it will be worth it."

"I know you're kidding, but I still like to believe it's an actual possibility. What do you need now?"

"The usual. A needle in a haystack." I explained what I needed, and April forwarded him the login information for her Multilancer account.

"How long will something like this take?" I asked.

"Tracing an IP address back? Not long."

"How not long?"

"This not long," he said. "Whoever FALCON4848 is, their server is in Boise."

"Anything more specific?"

"Now, that will take longer. Send you an address when I get one."

Boise. Hmm.

Before I left, Carlos shook my hand, and April gave me a hug.

"Thank you," she said. "What do you need from me?"

"First, I need you to call your Uncle Juan and let him know you're okay. I'll handle Stank for you. And I know this is going to be hard—for both of you—but you have to tell Juan about your dad."

"He'll be mad," April said.

"Yes. He will. At first. And then, eventually, he won't. Because he loves you. That's how it happens."

"And my involvement with the Knutsen?"

"I looked at your messages. You're a gifted teenager who got paid to paint a replica. Just because somebody else did a bad thing, it doesn't mean you did. I'm going to solve this case. And once I do, I'll find the right time to explain this to the sheriff."

"You're sure?"

"You don't want this hanging on your heart. It'll be too heavy. And trust me, this sheriff . . . he's one of the good guys."

It was getting dark as I drove out of the Sawtooth Forest back onto the highway. I was driving with no particular destination, like Jimmy and I would back in high school. We'd listen to the radio with the windows down. He'd wrap the fingers of his right hand together with the fingers of my left, and I'd let my right hand float out the window and pretend it was a bird riding along with the waves of the wind. We wouldn't say anything during those drives, but I've never felt closer to anybody in my life than in those moments.

Occasionally, I'd turn and look at this boy who loved me so much. And I'd just smile. And he'd always react the same.

"What?" he'd say with that beautiful mischievous grin.

I always answered the same way. "Nothing."

And then I'd wrap my hand just a little tighter around his.

And now here I was, back in Hopeless. I still hoped to find a job at a big-city newspaper, but it was also so good to be here. To be around Granny, Bess, and Katie. And tonight, the way April hugged me . . . I don't know. It felt good.

I felt my mind drifting someplace else. Someplace new. I wasn't thinking about a boy named Jimmy as much. Instead, I was thinking about a man named Alex.

I thought about what I had told April. Alex really *was* one of the good guys. I believed that. But I also knew that he was the sheriff . . . and a serious pain in my butt. I was certain he would say the same thing about me.

I let my hand float outside the window, riding the waves of the wind. And I wondered if maybe, just maybe, there was a chance for Alex and me.

A tingling went down my spine, and I shivered at the thought. And then I bit my lip.

I had no idea if Alex found himself thinking about me the way I did about him. I had no idea if there was any possibility for us. I did know he wasn't a big fan of me getting in his way. And he sure as heck wouldn't be happy about me holding back information as big as the true identity of the forger. But I couldn't rat April out. Not yet.

I pulled the car around, pointed it back toward Hopeless, and hit the gas. I needed to go back to the Library, set up my whiteboard, and figure out this puzzle.

I had a bet to win.

CHAPTER 26

When Bess and Granny came into the Library the next morning, I had the whiteboard set up in the middle of the bar and was already on my second pot of coffee.

"Not this again," Granny said. "Man, if you worked as hard at painting my house as you do at catching murderers . . ." Her voice trailed off.

"We'd have better painted houses, but also more murderers on the streets?"

"Okay, yeah, when you say it out loud like that, it sounds like you've got your priorities straight. So, who's your money on?"

"I've been over it a million times. I still don't know."

"But you've narrowed it down?"

"I think."

"And now you're just waiting for Bess and me to swoop down at the last second and solve it for you like we did last time, right?"

"I do believe it was Bess who did the swooping."

Granny shrugged. "A technicality."

I looked over at Bess. "You ready to talk again and solve this case for me too?"

Bess frowned, then started getting the bar ready for the day.

"Well, then," Granny said. "I guess it's up to Super Granny to solve this thing." She grabbed a mug, poured some of my coffee into it, and took a sip. Then she made a sour face. "You make the worst coffee in history." She reached over the bar, grabbed a bottle of bourbon, and added it to her coffee. This time she didn't sip—she chugged. "Now that's much better! Okay, granddaughter, bring me up to speed."

So I did. I started at the beginning and told her everything I knew about the case. When I finished, she took a long look at the whiteboard. She went to take another sip from her coffee mug, but it was empty, so she grabbed the bottle of bourbon and took a big swig of that instead.

"Okay," she said. "I got nothin'. In my defense, I'm old, and my brain doesn't work so well anymore."

"You think the half a bottle of bourbon you just chugged might have something to do with that?"

"Nonsense. Just go through them again. Start with your least likely theories."

"Okay. Theory number one—this was a professional art heist. Pimsey interrupts it. He gets killed."

"But that theory got nixed once the sheriff found the murder weapon in someone's bed," Granny said.

"Exactly. No way some stranger kills Pimsey and then takes the time to sneak into someone's room and hide the murder weapon."

"So it had to be an inside job. And you don't think there's any chance Juan did it?"

"I know nice people can do bad things, but Juan? I don't think so. Plus, the only thing he's been concerned about is his niece, April. *Plus* plus, he didn't have any particular dislike of Pimsey. *Plus* plus . . . uh, plus, he doesn't live at the house, and nobody has said anything that would point to him. Juan's off the list."

Granny made another sour face. "Yeah, that's a lot of pluses. Okay, then there's this Sokolov guy. From the auction place."

"Billingham's in San Francisco," I said. "On the one hand, since he runs in the art world, he'd be able to find a competent forger. On the other hand, he's the one who told us the painting was a forgery. Why would he do that if he's in on it? Why not just let everyone think Isabelle Thorndale's got the real Knutsen while he goes off into the sunset with the original? Nope. I don't think Sokolov did it."

Granny slapped her hands together. "And now it gets more interesting. Let's talk about the cook."

"Mrs. Schneider. It's definitely possible. She admitted that she never liked Pimsey much. She said he could be a bit of a bully. She even admitted to thinking about killing him a few times."

"I think I like this woman."

"But my gut says it wasn't her."

"Does that mean you've ruled her out?"

"I can't rule her out. But she's got no motive, not really. How often do people murder just because of general dislike?"

"Okay. Do the maid."

"Scratchett's got a real motive. The old gardener was a man named Rex Buttman. But *she* called him—"

"Sexy Rexy," Granny said with a big smile. "I remember him. He came in here all the time. Not bad-looking for a toothless guy."

"And Pimsey got rid of him. Broke Scratchett's heart. That's real motive. Plus, she's a tough, scrappy woman."

"But you don't think she did it."

"I don't. Why now? Pimsey fired Buttman years ago. And what would the painting have to do with it? Again, I can't rule her out, but I don't think it's her."

"I believe the creepy security guy is up next," Granny said.

"Ah, yes, Mortimer Snoot. As much fun as it was to kick him in the gremlins back in my youth, I don't think he's the guy."

"I know you're trusting your gut here, but the man does have some evidence stacked up against him. The sheriff found the murder weapon hidden in his mattress. And that little confession note that got slipped under the Library door just happens to match his handwriting."

"True and true, but doesn't that just seem too neat and tidy? It does to me. It feels like someone's setting him up. And since he's a rube, he's an easy guy to set up. And he's got a perfect alibi for when I was pushed off that balcony. He was in jail."

Granny nodded soberly as if she wouldn't mind getting her hand on whoever pushed me that night. "So, that brings us to the Thorndales. Who's up first?"

"Clay. Possible alcoholic, looks older than he is. Decent guy. Fairly charming. I don't think he did it."

"Because he took you out on your first date in twelve years."

"First of all, that was not a date. It was a fact-finding mission."

"Or maybe he was trying to win you over so you wouldn't consider him a suspect," Granny suggested. "Besides, he's a man. Men are usually the killers."

"But he puked as soon as he saw Pimsey dead. He told me he's not very good around blood. Not exactly the reaction of a stone-cold killer."

"Unless he was faking. And don't forget he's the one who showed you the secret passageway. The one where you almost got killed."

"But he was behind me, back in his mother's room. There's no way he pushed me off that balcony."

"He might have had an accomplice," Granny pointed out.

"You're right—that's a real possibility. Okay. Isabelle Thorndale."

"The old bat herself," Granny said.

"For starters, she's mean, and it seems no one would be surprised to learn that she killed somebody."

"What would be surprising is to learn that she'd only killed *one* person."

I tapped on the whiteboard with my marker. "The question is, why would she kill Pimsey? And why would she steal her own painting?"

"I don't know about the painting, but as for Pimsey . . . love can make you do crazy things. And they *were* in love, as you discovered when you stole Mrs. Thorndale's journal."

"Stole? I prefer 'found with extreme prejudice.' Yes, once upon a time Isabelle Thorndale was in love with Walter Pimsey. And they've fought like cats and dogs for years. So the passion was still there between them . . . in some form. Who knows?"

"Maybe Scratchett and Schneider were right," Granny said. "Maybe this latest fight was a big one. And Pimsey decided to go through with his plan to steal the Knutsen."

"And Mrs. Thorndale follows him, using Snoot's flashlight to light her way. She sees what Pimsey is doing, and conks him over the head. But because she loved him, she feels bad and slips the note under the Library door. But by the time she gets back to the house, she's in full cover-up mode."

"That theory makes sense, but it's a lot of maybes and mights," Granny said.

"I know. And that brings us to our final two suspects. The daughters. Valerie and Kitty Thorndale. Let's take Valerie first."

"What's her motive?"

"Here's a woman who got the bad end of a divorce and has had to claw her way back. She never got any financial help from her mother after she blew through her small trust fund. She's gotten back on her feet through hard work, but she admits it's exhausting. She could certainly use a break, financially speaking. So Valerie certainly had a motive to steal that painting. And if Pimsey got in her way, who knows what she would be capable of? Plus, she knew about the secret passageway.

She might have been the one who pushed me off the balcony."

"But why should she want to kill you?" Granny asked. "It's not like you've figured anything out yet. I mean, just being honest here."

"Thanks for the vote of confidence. Maybe she was following me. Maybe she thought I was getting close to something. Or maybe she was just in the passageway, saw me, and panicked. I've never been a murderer, so I'm not entirely sure how they think."

"Okay. Valerie seems like a good suspect," Granny said. "What about Kitty?"

"She actually had a good relationship with Pimsey, so that's a mark against her being the murderer. But then again, she absolutely hated her mother—it seems like the hate was mutual—so stealing the painting, her mother's most prized possession, would be a great way to strike out at her. But maybe Pimsey catches her in the act, and she just reacts and swings the flashlight. Maybe it was dark and she didn't even know who it was. Then when she saw she killed Pimsey . . . It would make total sense that she would feel guilty enough to leave a note that said, 'I didn't mean this to happen.'"

Granny narrowed her eyes at the whiteboard. "Okay. That's everyone. I think the evidence is most compelling for Snoot or Isabelle Thorndale."

"Not so fast—there's more evidence. First, we know that whoever planned this forgery hired April to do it. My man Darwin traced that person, Falcon 4848, to Boise. Both Valerie and Kitty live in Boise."

"Which one are you leaning toward?"

"Valerie. Kitty has an alibi. She was still in Boise the night of the murder. But Valerie was there all night."

"You really think it was Valerie?" Granny asked.

"Like I said, she could use a financial break. And if she did accidentally kill Pimsey, I could see her feeling bad enough to write that note. Plus she's a strong woman who knew about the secret passageway."

"Can you explain why she put the murder weapon in Snoot's mattress?"

"Yes. She wanted to frame him to throw the cops off her trail," I explained.

"And why does the handwriting on that note match Snoot's?"

"Same reason. Keep in mind, I'm not a professional analyst. The handwriting looks like Snoot's, but maybe she learned to mimic Snoot's. She's known him a long time."

Granny raised up on her tiptoes. "Well, the bourbon's making me pee. Don't solve this thing until I get back."

As she left for the restroom, my phone buzzed in my pocket. It was a text.

From Bess.

I looked over to the bar. Bess was on her phone. She waved to me frantically, then pointed at my phone. I read a new text that came in.

I heard what you said, but I don't really want to start talking again. Granny will give me way too much crap about it. I'm just going to text. You're wrong about Kitty.

"What do you mean, wrong?" I asked out loud as I stepped closer to the bar.

Bess shook her head and returned to her phone. I

received a new text.

Kitty wasn't in Boise that night. I remember. I was over at that new Bouncing Baby Billiards pool hall in Tourist Town. Don't tell Granny—she'll give me way too much crap about that too. Anyways, Kitty was there.

"Kitty was there that night? You're sure?"

Positive. She got super drunk, shoved a pool cue into a guy's ribs, and puked all over table 9. I don't know where she slept that night, but there's no way she was in any shape to get back to Boise.

"So she lied about where she was. Why would she do that?"

Bess shook her head. New text.

Same reason anybody lies about an alibi. They're guilty.

I reached over the bar and gave Bess a big hug.

"Thank you, Bess. Again."

"Thank you for what?" Granny asked, returning from the bathroom. "What did I miss?"

I turned to Granny and smiled. "I think we might have just solved the case."

As Granny gave Bess a bewildered look, my phone buzzed again. It wasn't from Bess. It was from Darwin.

I read it over and smiled. He had found the approximate address in Boise for Multilancer user Falcon4848. He'd even compared it to Valerie's and Kitty's addresses.

The address belonged to a coffee shop that was six blocks from Valerie's apartment.

But only *one* block away from Kitty's apartment.

"Correction," I said as I jogged out of the Library's front door and dialed Alex's number. "I think we *definitely* solved the case."

CHAPTER 27

When I arrived at the Thorndales' mansion, Sheriff Kramer was in the circular drive escorting Clay Thorndale and Kitty into the house. Suitcases were stacked up next to Clay's car. It appeared that Clay and Kitty had been going somewhere—and had been prevented from leaving by the sheriff.

I followed them into the Thorndales' lavish great room, where the entire household, staff and family alike, had been assembled.

Kitty looked terrible. Red splotches covered her face—at least the part of it that wasn't shielded by large sunglasses. Clay stood with his arms folded, looking angry and checking his watch, like he needed to be somewhere. Isabelle Thorndale, as always, looked highly annoyed. Of the Thorndale family, only Valerie looked calm and under control, her face betraying nothing.

The hour bell sounded on the stately grandfather clock. It was nine a.m.

Time to uncover the truth.

"Sheriff Kramer, what exactly are we doing here?" Isabelle asked.

"According to Miss Walker, there's been a development in the case."

Mrs. Scratchett scrunched her face. "A development? I thought the case was closed."

"Yeah," Clay said. "I thought Mr. Snoot did it."

"His flashlight was the murder weapon, right?" Mrs. Schneider said.

Alex nodded. "That's true."

"And that confession note was written by him, right?" Juan asked. Apparently, word had gotten around if even Juan knew every detail of our gathered evidence.

"We've sent the note away to the FBI for handwriting analysis. It'll take time to get the results back, but at first glance, yes, it looks like a match."

"Then what are we doing here?" Isabelle snapped.

"Well, for one thing, we have yet to find your painting, Mrs. Thorndale."

"Only because you haven't done your job and gotten the truth out of Snoot."

"You mean I haven't tortured him yet?"

Isabelle shook her head in disgust. "It's only you namby-pamby liberals who call it torture. Where I come from, it's called '*persuasion*.'"

"Oh, come off it, Mother," Valerie said. "You're from Salt Lake City. They don't call it persuasion in Salt Lake City." She faced Alex, then looked at me. "So, what have you learned?"

I was about to speak when the sheriff cut me off. "Actually, I learned a few things."

"*You* did?" I said in surprise.

"Yes, Hope. I'm the sheriff. It's my job to learn things." He winked and lowered his voice to a whisper. "And I'm not about to lose a bet."

He cleared his throat. "At first glance, it appears that Mortimer Snoot is the man behind these terrible crimes. But I have to be honest, from the beginning, it never felt right. If you've spent more than one minute with the man, you realize he's a dimly lit witless fool."

"I've been saying that for years," Isabelle muttered.

"We've all been thinking it for years," Mrs. Scratchett cracked.

"And since he's been staying in my jail cell for the last few days, I've spent more than a minute with the man. I'm telling you, he's no criminal mastermind. You're telling me that he figured out how to forge a valuable painting, kill a man, and hide the painting . . . but then somehow he hides the bloody murder weapon in his own bed and writes a confession note that he slips under the door of the local bar? No. I don't buy any of that for a second. From the beginning, it was clear to me that somebody was trying to frame Mortimer Snoot."

Alex paced back and forth in front of the assembled group. I could tell that he and his unnaturally green eyes were suddenly making them uncomfortable. Then suddenly he stopped.

"The question is, which one of you wanted Snoot framed, a million-dollar painting in your hands, and Pimsey dead? And even though plenty of you disliked Pimsey, and *all* of you could stand to make a few million dollars off a stolen painting, I kept coming back to one name."

He began pacing again, but this time he stopped in front of one particular person. Clay Thorndale.

"Me?" Clay asked.

"Yes, you," said the sheriff. "With all the hard evidence in this case pointing to Mortimer Snoot, I thought it best to look hard at *motive*. As I said, everybody in this room could benefit from a few million extra dollars. But who, I asked myself, absolutely *needed* that kind of money?"

Clay suddenly looked very uncomfortable.

"You know what I'm talking about, don't you, Clay?"

"Clay?" Valerie asked. "What's this about?"

"I'm talking about his business in Malibu—his surfboard company," Alex said. "I did some digging. It seems creditors and investors are breathing down your neck, Clay. I even talked to some of your partners in Malibu and asked them why you didn't just file for bankruptcy. They told me you said, 'Bankruptcy is not an option.' That you're afraid of what your mother would think if your business failed. I asked them how much money your company needs to clear up its debts." Alex glanced back at me, then faced Clay once more. "Four million dollars. That's what you need."

"You're out of your mind!" Clay said.

"I'm not even done. That piece of information is damning enough—but then Valerie told me about the Thorndale Challenge."

Valerie had mentioned something about a Thorndale Challenge to me, too. Back at the party. But she'd never told me what it was, and I'd forgotten all about it.

"What are you talking about?" I asked.

"Oh, you don't know about the challenge?" Alex said with a smirk. "I don't think Valerie *wanted* to tell me about it—it seems the challenge is one of those old Thorndale secrets. But it's pretty simple. Only *one* of the children will inherit Mrs. Thorndale's estate upon her death. The other two get nothing."

Silence fell over the room.

"And Clay told his partner there was no way he or Kitty were going to win the competition. The inheritance would go to Valerie."

"Is this true, Valerie?" I asked.

She glanced at her mother and nodded. "Yeah, it's true. Mother told us about the challenge when we were young. She said the money would go to the child who was 'most worthy of carrying on the Thorndale name.'"

I turned to Isabelle. "Most *worthy*? What kind of challenge is that? How could you do that to your own children?"

"Oh, don't get your panties in a bunch. I did it to make them tough. My husband and I didn't build all this by having it *handed* to us. I wanted to make sure my children learned a strong work ethic."

"And is it true that Valerie is the one who will get your inheritance?" I asked.

"The challenge isn't over until I'm dead—and I'm not dead yet. So I'm not saying a word." She looked at Alex. "Sheriff, do you really think my Clay killed Pimsey?"

Alex bit his lip. "That's the way it's looking to me."

"Interesting. Because that's not the way it's looking to *me*," I said.

Alex shook his head, took his hat off, and ran a hand through his hair. "Okay, Hope. I guess it's your turn. Just don't make me regret this."

I turned away from the sheriff and cast my gaze over the assembled group. "I looked at all of you as suspects as well," I said. "Heck, for a while, I thought it might be Isabelle Thorndale."

She looked deeply offended. "Me?"

"Yes, you. Everybody I spoke to thought you were more than capable of killing someone, and *extra* capable of killing Pimsey."

"Well, I never!"

"How about *you* not get your panties in a bunch? Relax, old woman. Ultimately, I zeroed in on someone else."

Now it was my turn to be dramatic. I walked down the line, passing everyone in turn, eyeing each one closely, then backtracked . . . and stopped in front of Kitty Thorndale.

"Me?" she said, her voice seemingly caught in her throat.

"Yes, Kitty, you. And Sheriff Kramer just supplied the final piece to the puzzle. If there really was a competition to see who would get the inheritance, well, the winner certainly wouldn't be you. You and your mother have been estranged for years. Your room hasn't been lived in for years. Your mutual contempt for each other is obvious. So you definitely had motive. But motive alone isn't enough to prove your guilt. There needed to be more. And I found more."

I backed up and addressed everyone. "Ladies and gentlemen, I know the identity of the art forger."

Alex did a double take. "Wait, what? You know?"

"Yes. The forger was hired via an electronic transaction so the client could remain anonymous. But with the help of a very smart person, I was able to trace where that transaction was initiated—Boise. Specifically, a coffee shop less than one block from . . ."

I looked at Kitty.

". . . your apartment."

The group certainly reacted to that piece of information.

"That doesn't prove anything," Kitty said.

"Really? How about this—the day we discovered Pimsey, everybody was at the house. You arrived a little bit after we found him. You freaked out. Sobbing and wailing. Nobody else reacted that way. Later on, I wondered why. And then I learned that you were an actress. Community theater and all. Was it possible you were acting?"

Kitty's mouth fell open. "How dare you?"

I ignored her outburst. "And as for your alibi? Originally, I ruled you out as a suspect because I was told you stayed in Boise the night before. Which made sense. You never stay here. I saw your room—it's empty. I assume you stayed there last night, perhaps to keep an eye on the investigation. But as for the night of the murder? You had no reason to be in Hopeless. None whatsoever."

Kitty got a guilty look on her face and looked at Clay for support.

"However . . . you *didn't* stay in Boise that night, did

you?" I said. "I learned this morning that you were, in fact, making quite a scene down at Bouncing Baby Billiards. Gave someone a pool cue to the ribs? Puked all over table 9? Ring any bells? By the way, you and Clay should get control of this puking tendency.

"But my point is, you were in no shape to return to Boise that night. Which means you lied. Your alibi is fake. And Kitty, you know who lies about an alibi? Guilty people, that's who."

Kitty's lower lip trembled.

"Kitty," I said. "Does everyone here know about the secret passageway?"

"Wait. How do you know about that?"

"I know that somebody in that passageway tried to kill me. But it wasn't you, was it?"

Her eyes widened. "No!"

"And as for your reaction to Pimsey's death, yes, it might have been acting. But I suspect it was genuine."

"Of *course* it was genuine. I . . ." She stopped herself.

"You loved him, didn't you?"

Kitty looked at the floor. Her voice shook. "Yes. I loved him very much."

"I knew it. Now it all makes sense."

"What does?"

"The fight between Pimsey and your mother. The night before the party. Pimsey told your mother about you and him. It was an unconventional relationship, but after all, you do have a history of being involved with older men."

"What? No!"

"You and Pimsey had a plan, didn't you? The money

from the stolen painting would allow the two of you to run away together. Pimsey knew of someone who might be qualified to do it, but you're the one who contacted the forger and made the arrangements. And then, just as soon as Sokolov authenticated the painting, Pimsey told your mother the truth about your relationship."

"No! You're wrong!"

"And your mother was angry. Not angry enough to kill Pimsey, but angry enough to finally tell you the truth. The truth she had hidden from you and your siblings forever."

"What truth?" Valerie asked. "What are you talking about?"

"Once upon a time, your mother and Pimsey were in love."

CHAPTER 28

"What?" Clay yelled. Kitty covered her mouth. Valerie shrieked, and one of the women behind me gasped.

"And when you discovered the man you loved had once had an affair with your mother, you lost your mind. He'd never told you this. You felt betrayed. And you killed him."

Kitty broke down in tears. Clay wrapped her in his arms and held her. Alex looked at me in shock. In fact, the whole room seemed to be in considerable shock. The only sound in the room was Kitty's sobs.

Then she broke free from Clay, turned to me, and looked me in the eye. Her face was streaked with tears, but her jaw was set. "No!" She poked me in the chest. "No! I did *not* do this!"

"Then how do you—?"

She poked me again. "First, I learned many years ago not to give a *rip* about this family's money. Money is poisonous, and I'm *sick* of it. I don't care about the Thorndale Challenge, and I sure as hell don't care about that ugly painting. Second, I know the coffee shop you're talking about near my house. And news flash—I never go there. Never! I don't care what you have to do. Give me a polygraph, interview the employees, whatever, but I've never even gone inside. And lastly and most importantly, I did *not* have an affair with Pimsey. I have never been more offended in my entire life. You're right, I was close to him. I always have been. But not because I was having an affair with him. What's wrong with you? Walter Pimsey wasn't my lover—he was my *friend*. No, that's not right either. Walter Pimsey was more like . . . a father to me."

I had to admit, Kitty Thorndale sounded sincere. But I also had to remember, she was an actress. And there was still a problem.

"Then why did you lie about your alibi?"

She put her head down. Clay patted her on the back, and she looked back up. First at me, then at everyone.

"For one simple reason. I was embarrassed about the scene I'd made at the billiards hall. And I'm tired of disappointing my mother. I don't care about the money or her stupid challenge, but I care about her. I actually care about that miserable woman. And all I've ever been is a giant disappointment to her. You see, I'm a drunk. An alcoholic. I have a problem."

Clay cleared his throat. "And I have a problem too. I thought I could manage it on my own . . . and some days I can. But I have to stop drinking."

"But the bags out by the car?" I said. "It looks like you and Clay were in some kind of hurry to leave."

"I'm not fleeing the country, if that's what you're

suggesting. Clay was going to drive me to a rehab center in Sun Valley. I'm going to get the help I've needed for a long time. I couldn't do it alone."

"So I'm going with her," Clay said. "We're going to do it together."

"Is this true?" Alex asked.

Clay nodded. He pulled out his phone, scrolled through it, then showed it to the sheriff. "This is a confirmation email from Dr. Hastings at Mount Pleasant Treatment Center. We're expected at ten thirty this morning."

Alex read the email, then looked up at Clay. His voice was gentle. "I know a thing or two about rehab," he said. "And I know it's important to go in with a clean slate, if you can. So I have to ask—did either of you have anything to do with Pimsey or the painting? Do you know anything about it at all?"

Clay and Kitty exchanged a look. Then Clay answered. "What you found out about my company is true. We screwed up, got overleveraged, and I thought I could figure it out, but I couldn't. I was an incompetent lawyer, and I guess I'm also an incompetent surfboard exec. So could I have used the money? Sure. But I had nothing to do with this."

"And neither did I," Kitty said defiantly. "Pimsey was my friend. He was prickly to most people, but never to me. He was always kind to me. Always. He treated me more like a daughter than my real father ever did."

"Now, Sheriff," Clay said, "if you need to reach us sometime in the next thirty days, you know where to find us. But this has been beyond upsetting, and if there's nothing else, we really need to go."

"Of course," Alex said. "You're both free to leave. And if I have more questions, I'll know where to find you."

Clay and Kitty walked out together, and that somehow signaled the end of this little get-together. Scratchett and Schneider and Juan all went their separate ways.

That left me alone with the sheriff, Valerie, and Isabelle.

Valerie looked furious. "Are you happy, Mother?"

"What? How is this *my* fault?"

"You are unbelievable. You and your sham of a marriage. You and this stupid big house. You and your ugly painting and your idiotic parties and worst of all, you and your horrible Thorndale Challenge. Your daughter and your son just walked out of here *hurting*. They need their family. And by God, in case you didn't notice, you are their freaking *mother*. What if, for once in your miserable life, you start acting like it?"

Valerie charged out of the room.

I never thought I'd see Isabelle Thorndale completely speechless, but at that moment, I did. I thought she'd lash out at me, or Alex, or at the world. She didn't. She just walked out of the room like a zombie. I heard her on the stairs, and I couldn't help but think she was headed for her whiskey, her pills, and her bed.

"Well, that went poorly," I said.

"'Poorly' is an understatement," Alex said. "It was horrifying. And embarrassing as hell. The evidence says Mortimer Snoot is our man, and I should have listened to the evidence instead of listening to you."

"But doesn't it bother you that we haven't found the painting?"

"Of course it does. And we'll keep looking. And so will the insurance company."

"What do we do until then?"

"We don't do anything, Hope. I should have never agreed to this stupid bet."

"But you did."

"Not anymore."

"You can't do that."

"Watch me. What you call 'following the story,' I call guessing. And yes, sometimes you get lucky. But at what cost?"

"That's not fair!"

"Yes, it is. I am a sheriff. What I do is police work. I follow procedure. What *you* do is a lot of guessing. I don't have that luxury. I have to build a case so that a prosecutor can convince a jury that someone is guilty. Beyond a reasonable doubt. Now, I'm going back to my office to get Mortimer Snoot ready for transport to state police custody. And you, Hope—I'm begging you—please, just go home."

CHAPTER 29

There I was in the Thorndales' massive great room. Surrounded by rugs and couches and chairs and sculptures and paintings and a grand old grandfather clock. Everything put there for no purpose other than to show off what had been accumulated through a lifetime of excess.

And I felt very alone.

I hated the way Alex had talked to me, like I was a child. The fact was, I was the one who had solved the murders of Sheriff Kline and Patrick Crofton. I was the one who had been here at the Thorndale house from the beginning. When the butler had been found. When the fake painting had been discovered. I had gone through every conceivable permutation of who might be involved in these crimes and why.

But the puzzle hadn't come together.

And the worst part . . .

The worst part was that Alex was right. I was guessing.

I knew in my gut that I didn't have it right. Didn't have

all the pieces yet. But I'd wanted to win that stupid bet. And so I had guessed, just *hoping* to be right.

The facts of the case said that Mortimer Snoot committed the murder of Walter Pimsey. There was the murder weapon. There was the paper confession. And if the FBI analysts looked at the samples and concluded the handwriting was a match, that would probably be case closed.

I sure wish the FBI wasn't so slow. I mean, how hard can it be for an expert to look at two samples of handwriting and determine whether they match? That art expert Anton Sokolov had looked at that painting for less than a minute before he figured out it was a fake.

Wasn't handwriting analysis basically the same thing?

Too bad I didn't have Sokolov's phone number. Maybe he could look at the handwriting for me.

But then I remembered something. I did know an art expert. Who better to figure out if something was real or fake than an artist who could do a little of both?

I found the photos I'd taken of the confession note and the handwriting sample from Snoot's room. I texted them both to April, and I asked her a simple question.

Is the handwriting the same?

And then I waited.

And while I waited, I thought about what had happened in this room just now. I buried my head in my hands. Alex was right about that, too. It was embarrassing. I had accused Kitty of having an affair with a much older dead man. A man who had been a father figure to her. She seemed genuinely horrified by the suggestion.

I think *everyone* had been horrified by the suggestion.

Just like April looked horrified when I thought Carlos was her boyfriend.

As a reporter, you learn to get a read on people. And my read told me that Kitty was telling the truth.

My phone buzzed, and I took it out. The message was one word long.

No.

My heart thumped in my chest. I texted April back.

Are you sure?

April: 100% sure.

Me: Nobody's 100% sure of anything.

April: I am. Trust me. The note is a fake. A forgery. I would know.

So I was right. The evidence *was* wrong. Snoot *didn't* do it. And the events of this morning had convinced me that Clay and Kitty didn't do it either.

Who was left?

I quickly went through everyone once more. I thought about what each one of them was hiding. I could pick out the most likely suspect, but . . .

Well, I'd just be guessing.

Alex was right.

Law enforcement officers followed procedure for a reason. You can't just go around pointing fingers. Before you put someone in jail, you need proof.

You need evidence.

And evidence was in short supply in this case.

But I reviewed what I had. I looked only at cold, hard facts. Actual physical evidence.

Mortimer Snoot's flashlight. The murder weapon, according to blood analysis.

The note. A fake.

And the Knutsen. Also a fake.

I sighed. We had nothing.

We'd searched the entire house and grounds, and sure, we'd found the murder weapon, but no painting. And no clues. Unless you counted all the hairs and fibers and things Alex had collected. But what would those prove? The suspects had been all over the house—most of them lived there. Naturally there would be traces of them everywhere. Alex had gotten DNA samples from everyone, just in case, but . . .

It was worth asking.

I took out my phone and texted Katie. *Anything come up from the DNA samples?*

First, I heard Hurricane Hope just made an appearance. Second, I'm not supposed to talk to you. Third, Alex told me to use a poop emoji to get the message across. Fourth, state homicide lab said results not back till tomorrow. And no, he doesn't know I'm telling you that.

You're the worst.

No, you are.

I thought for a moment. Then I remembered—no woman ever accomplished anything in this world by asking a man's permission first. I found the number to the state homicide headquarters, and I asked for the number to the crime lab.

"Crime lab. Jergens speaking."

"This is Katie Rodgers over at Sheriff Kramer's office. Just wondering about the DNA samples on the Thorndale case."

"Thought I told you they wouldn't be ready till tomorrow."

"What can I say? The crossword was easy today, and the sheriff's breathing down my neck."

"So that badge is getting to Alex's head?"

"You have no idea."

"Well, Katie, you're in luck. We got the samples in earlier than I thought, and the results are in. Want me to email them over?"

"That would be great. But I don't necessarily speak DNA, so between you and me, did anything turn up?"

"Not really. The sheriff will need to do his own examination, but it just confirmed what you knew. Snoot's DNA was on the flashlight, and we found the presence of latex."

"Somebody was wearing gloves."

"That would be my guess."

"And nothing else?"

"If you're looking for a smoking gun, I'm sorry to disappoint you. But there was something weird."

"Weird how?"

"Nobody told me the butler and Mrs. Thorndale were married."

"Wait. What are you talking about?"

"So they *weren't* married. Then yeah, I'd say things just got a whole lot more interesting."

"You're going to need to explain what you're talking about," I said.

"We noticed it when we were looking at the DNA samples. All three Thorndale children share familial DNA with their mother, Isabelle. Naturally. What we didn't expect was to find that one of those children also shares familial DNA with the butler, Pimsey. The youngest Thorndale. Kitty."

"You're saying . . ."

"The butler is Kitty's father."

* * *

I ENDED the call and stood there, trying to process what I'd just heard. Pimsey wasn't just a father *figure* to Kitty.

He *was* her father.

Wow.

Pimsey had an affair with Isabelle Thorndale years before. That much we knew. I'd never even considered that a child might have resulted from it.

I walked over to a table with family photos on it. There was one in particular I was interested in. A photo from about fifteen years prior. The family and the help, all together in one picture.

I looked at Isabelle. At her youngest daughter, Kitty.

At Mr. Thorndale.

And at Pimsey.

It was strange, really. Take the butler's tuxedo off him and put a proper tweed suit in its place, and Pimsey and Mr. Thorndale bore an eerie resemblance. Maybe that was why Isabelle had fallen for him in the first place. And no doubt that was how Isabelle had been able to keep her deepest and darkest secret for so many years.

Kitty Thorndale was Walter Pimsey's daughter.

I wondered if Mr. Thorndale ever figured it out.

Pimsey probably knew. It would explain was he was always so kind to Kitty. So fatherly to her.

I wondered if Kitty knew too, somewhere deep down.

And it made me wonder what, if anything, this had to do with a dead butler and a stolen piece of art.

"You finally figured it out, didn't you?"

I spun around to find Mrs. Scratchett, arms folded, eyeing me curiously.

"Figured out what?"

"You're looking at that picture awful closely. And you're thinking the same thing I've thought a thousand times before. 'My, don't Pimsey and Kitty look an awful bit alike.'"

"So you know?"

"That Pimsey is Kitty's father? Yeah."

"How long?"

"I've suspected since she was little. Though honestly, I've never known for sure."

"Pimsey never said."

"Nope. But you pretty well confirmed it."

"How do you mean?"

"I mean, you revealed that Mrs. Thorndale and Pimsey had an affair."

"That surprised you?"

"Oh, not in the least. Like I said, I've suspected for years."

"But you let out a gasp like you were surprised. I heard it. Right behind me."

"That wasn't me. That was Mrs. Schneider. She was right next to me. She may have been surprised, but for me, it was just confirmation of what I've always believed."

"Mrs. Schneider's been here a long time. Why was she surprised if you weren't?"

Mrs. Scratchett shrugged. "Hannah's a funny old bird. She runs her kitchen and reads her books and has her own opinions about things. I wasn't in her confidence. Not ever. But I think . . . I think once upon a time, she was sweet on Pimsey."

"Was?"

"Glimpses is all I saw. And then a few weeks ago, after all those years of glimpses and keeping to herself, it changed. She opened up. Turns out maybe I was wrong about her all along. Maybe she never liked him."

"Maybe?"

"Like I said, she's a funny old bird. You'd have to ask her for herself."

"And where is she?"

"Where she always is. In the kitchen."

CHAPTER 30

As I walked down the creepy dungeon staircase to the kitchen, I was wondering if this was the missing piece of the puzzle that would finally help things fall into place. If not, I was out of leads.

I found Mrs. Schneider at the kitchen sink, washing pots and pans. When she noticed me, she startled.

"Oh, Miss Walker. Can I help you?"

"Just a quick question. I was talking with Mrs. Scratchett upstairs, and she suggested I come talk to you."

"What about?"

"Did you know that Walter Pimsey was Kitty Thorndale's real father?"

Mrs. Schneider dropped her pan into the sink, and water splashed all over her apron.

Yep, things were about to fall in place all right.

"What did you say?" she said.

"I said that Walter Pimsey was Kitty Thorndale's biological father. You didn't know?"

"I . . . I . . ."

Mrs. Schneider was trembling, her whole body shaking. I didn't know what that meant, but I knew it meant something.

"Forgive me, Mrs. Schneider, but I noticed something earlier. When I revealed Mrs. Thorndale's big secret, that she and Pimsey had once been in love, I heard a gasp . . . like surprise. It came from a woman behind me. I asked Mrs. Scratchett if that was her, and she said no. She said she'd always suspected that Mrs. Thorndale had had an affair with Pimsey, and that Pimsey was Kitty's father. She said that you were the one who gasped—that you were the one who was surprised. And judging by your reaction just now, you still are."

"Well," she stammered, "I suppose I am. You work with someone that long . . . you think you know them."

"You sure it's not more than that?"

"What do you mean?"

"Mrs. Scratchett said something else. She said that once upon a time, she thought you were sweet on Mr. Pimsey."

Mrs. Schneider's lips twitched. "Sweet?"

"She couldn't be sure. She said you keep to yourself. But women, they can usually tell. And then a month ago, something changed. You started opening up to her. Told her how much you disliked Pimsey. In fact, you told me the same thing. And you know . . . that's an odd thing to offer someone who's questioning you about a murdered man. Most people wouldn't say anything that would make them more of a suspect. But you actually came right out and said you'd thought about killing him."

"Is there a question in there somewhere?"

"Yes, Mrs. Schneider. Did you like Mr. Pimsey? Romantically? And if so, what changed a month ago?"

"Nothing changed a month ago because none of what Mrs. Scratchett said is true."

"So you didn't have feelings for him?"

"I'm not a kindergartener. I'm a grown woman. And I do not need a man."

"I didn't ask if you needed a man. I asked if you *liked* a man. This man. Walter Pimsey. A man you've worked with for years. A man who, even though he's dead, when you found out he's the father of Kitty Thorndale, massively upset you."

"I think you should leave."

"Did you have feelings for him, Mrs. Schneider? It's a simple question."

"I don't have to answer your questions."

"No, you don't. But wouldn't you like to? You're shut up in this kitchen all the time, living this life of serving people. And what if, in the midst of it, there was a man. A man you had feelings for. A man who's now gone. Wouldn't you want to talk about that with someone?"

"You should leave."

"I won't leave until you answer the question. Did you like—?"

"*No!*" she screamed. "I didn't like him. I *loved* him! *I loved him!*"

She was really shaking now. Her face was a tortured mess of emotion—pain and anger and sadness. Deep sadness.

And all at once, things really did start to fit together.

"That's it. You loved him."

Yes. Now it made perfect sense. Occam's razor. The simplest explanation is probably correct.

"We found Pimsey by the fake Knutsen," I said. "The simplest explanation for him being there? He had something to do with stealing the painting. But why? Why after all those years would he steal the painting now?"

I smiled.

"Why do men do the most foolish things in their lives? For the women they love. Walter Pimsey was stealing that painting for the woman he loved. You.

"Or at least . . . you *thought* you were the woman he loved. Until a month ago, when something changed. You discovered he loved *another* woman. Kitty Thorndale. Young. Beautiful. You could never compete with her. You had been betrayed. And you hatched a plan.

"First you started spreading rumors that you didn't like him. You wanted it to seem like that was what you were hiding. You wanted us to discover that, as if that was your dark secret. We would never suspect the person who offered up their dislike as if they had nothing to hide. Am I right?"

Mrs. Schneider's hands were tied up in her apron. She was shaking badly now. And that's when I spotted her calendar on the wall behind her. A word jumped out at me. *Boise*. Every Saturday, the words "*Boise: shopping*" were written on her calendar.

"It was you!" I said. "You arranged the forgery on Multilancer.net. We thought it was Valerie or Kitty, since they live in Boise. No doubt that was also part of your plan. You threw suspicion on them just like you threw suspicion on Snoot. You didn't care who got hurt as long as it wasn't you. You even tried to kill me in that secret passageway.

"But it wasn't *only* you. You and Pimsey were in on this together. Pimsey was going to steal a painting for his beloved. You assumed it was you! You helped him out. You got the forgery. But then you found out about Kitty. I don't know what you saw, or what you heard, but you jumped to the same conclusion I did, that Pimsey and Kitty were having an affair. And just like that, you went from the beloved to the scorned. And I'm guessing Hannah Schneider is not a woman to be messed with. Are you?"

Mrs. Schneider was no longer shaking. She was calm. And quiet.

"You waited for your chance. Your chance for revenge. You knew when Pimsey would switch the paintings. Of course you did—you were in on the plan. So you just hid in the darkness. And when Pimsey let himself in that night with the fake painting, you followed him with Snoot's flashlight, and boom, you killed him. You switched out the paintings, grabbed his key, locked up, and left with the real painting. Your revenge was complete.

"Except now you've learned you were wrong. Horribly wrong. Walter Pimsey wasn't having an affair with Kitty Thorndale. He loved her, yes—because she was his daughter. And you killed him."

Mrs. Schneider set her fierce gray eyes on me.

"It's a clever story, Miss Walker. It really is. But that's all it is—a story. If you were hoping you would scare me into a confession, I don't scare easily. And as far as I can tell, the only evidence you've got of *anything* is a murder weapon belonging to Mr. Snoot and a confession note in his handwriting."

"Oh, yes, the note's a fake. I just found that out. I'm sure we'll discover you're the one who wrote it soon enough."

"I very much doubt that. No, if you had anything more than a clever story, I wouldn't have an annoying reporter in my kitchen bothering me with fiction. I'd have a sheriff showing up with handcuffs to arrest me."

"You're very smooth, Mrs. Schneider. I'll give you that. But you mentioned evidence. And it seems like there's only one piece of evidence that really matters in this case. The painting. The *real* painting. There's only one problem. We've been through the entire house, and we didn't find it. But I'm not sure I was thinking about it right. I was wondering where *someone* might hide a painting. But that's different from asking where *you* would hide a painting.

"Mrs. Scratchett says you almost never leave the kitchen. And as far as I know, you haven't left the house since the murder. So it's safe to say the painting is here. In the kitchen."

"Now you're just making a fool out of yourself. You and your friend already searched this kitchen."

"That we did. That we did . . . "

I was running out of steam. We had thoroughly searched this kitchen. We'd looked everywhere, and had found nothing. But I knew now, the painting *had* to be here. That Mrs. Schneider *must* have hidden it here.

Where would a cook, a baker, hide a painting . . . where nobody would look?

I snapped my fingers. *Of course.*

I looked at Mrs. Schneider. I knew where the painting was.

And she knew I knew.

"When we started our search, Sheriff Kramer told us to be on the lookout for anything suspicious. And when I entered your kitchen the day after the big party, there *was* something suspicious—you were frosting a big sheet cake. That was odd. Why bake a big cake *after* the party is finished? But to be honest, I didn't give it much thought. Perhaps you were baking ahead for the next event. That's what Bess used to do. Bake her cakes ahead of time and then freeze them.

"But now I know that wasn't it at all. It wasn't about the cake. I remember thinking that the Knutsen is about the size of a laptop. And you know what else is about the size of a laptop? A sheet cake pan."

Mrs. Schneider's eyes widened. "Do you really think I *baked* a valuable painting?"

"I think you baked a cake the same size as that painting, then hid the painting under the cake when it was done. Then you frosted it and put it in the freezer. You knew the police would be searching high and low, and you knew that was the one place they would never, ever look."

Mrs. Schneider let loose an uncomfortable laugh. "You sound more like a fantasy author than a reporter."

"Well, there's one easy way to prove me wrong."

"You want to look under my cake?"

"Seems a fairly easy way to clear yourself of murder."

Mrs. Schneider's face twisted. "And when you find no painting, do you promise to leave and never bother me again?"

"Of course."

"Fine." She shook her head in annoyance, then opened the door to the freezer and ushered me forth to take a look.

The sheet cake was on a rack near the bottom of the freezer. It was wrapped in foil. I grabbed the cold pan with both hands, slid it out of the rack, picked up the cake, and turned to take it back to the kitchen table.

By the time I saw the rolling pin coming at me, I had only enough time to drop the cake and raise my arm. The pin blasted my arm and caught me in the side of the head.

And everything went dark.

CHAPTER 31

I woke up in a chair with my hands tied behind me. My right arm screamed in pain. My head was worse, the inside of my skull thump-thump-thumping away. I was dizzy and felt like I was going to throw up.

I opened my eyes. I was in the kitchen. Mrs. Schneider was standing at the table, where a busted-up cake was scattered about. A duffel bag and suitcase sat beside her.

She pulled a clear plastic bag from the cake pan. Inside the bag was the Knutsen. The *real* Knutsen.

"I was a little worried about the painting being frozen," she said in a surprisingly jolly tone. "But it doesn't look any worse for wear." She held it up so I could see. "It's really an ugly painting, don't you think?"

"It's awful," I said.

"And yet it's worth millions of dollars. Funny, eh?"

She slipped the painting into her suitcase, then pulled out her passport and waved it at me. "Got my passport, a little spending money, and a very expensive ugly painting that will provide for my retirement. And in twelve hours, I'll be on a beach in Mexico where nosy reporters like you will never be able to find me."

"I'll find you."

"Oh, no, dear, you won't. You'll be dead."

Now I *really* felt like I was going to throw up. "You'll never get away with it."

"Get away with it? I'll have enough money to hide for the rest of my life. I will most definitely get away with it."

She poured whiskey into a glass, then pulled a bottle of sleeping pills from her pocket. "I can see you're in a lot of pain, Hope. Some whiskey and some sleeping pills will make the pain go away."

I tried to get my fingers around the rope that bound my wrists, but it was tied too tight. I had to get a fingernail in there, loosen it up. I needed to buy time.

"You don't have to kill me."

"No, that's where you're wrong. I have to clean up my messes. And you are a mess. The person I didn't *have* to kill was my beloved Walter. I'm very sorry about that. I really did love him. I loved him for years. And when he told me about his plan to steal the painting to make a future for his best girl—that was the term he used, 'best girl'—I naturally assumed he meant me."

"So the two of you were romantic?"

"Not in the way you probably mean. But the way we were with each other . . . there was an understanding. It was old-fashioned, maybe, but I wasn't making it up."

"And then you found out who he meant by his best girl."

"That damned Kitty Thorndale. I was the one who

helped him think through how to steal the painting, and then this gorgeous rich girl swoops in to steal *my* man?"

"Except she wasn't swooping in to steal your man. He was her father."

"Which makes what I did rather unfortunate."

"*Unfortunate*? You killed him."

"By mistake. But I can't go back and undo it now. All I can do is clean up my messes."

"That's what I am? Not a person. Just a mess."

"Once again, it's unfortunate. For you. Okay, no more stalling." She dropped a large handful of pills into the whiskey and shook it up.

I screamed as loudly as I could.

All Mrs. Schneider did was smile. "Dear, this basement is made of eight-inch-thick rock. Trust me, nobody can hear anything down here."

"If you come near me with those pills, I'll bite your finger off."

"You're going to make this difficult, aren't you? Well, I didn't want to make this messy, but a good bop on the head should make you think twice."

She grabbed a heavy pan in one hand. With her other, she held the pill-laced whiskey. I fought like mad to get that knot to come undone. But it was no use.

I had run out of time.

And then, for some reason, for the very first time, I noticed my feet.

She hadn't tied my feet to the chair.

I planted my feet as firmly against the concrete floor as I could. I looked her right in the eyes.

She held up her pan and said, "I really am sorry it had to come to this."

I launched myself and that chair off the ground, put my head down, and rammed it into her stomach with everything I had. I drove her up and back, right into the refrigerator. Once I had her there, I kept ramming my head into her belly until finally, when I backed up, she slumped over onto the floor.

And then I did the only thing I could think to do. I sat my chair over her, straddling her, creating a jail cell that I hoped she couldn't get out of.

After a couple of minutes, her breath came back, and her screaming began. She fought like hell to get out.

But as long as my big butt was glued to that chair, she was a prisoner. She was *my* prisoner.

"Remember, Mrs. Schneider, this basement is made of eight-inch-thick rock. Trust me, nobody can hear anything down here."

And though it took me another twenty minutes to untie the knot around my wrists, I finally did. I used that same rope to tie her feet together. Then I took off my belt and tied her hands together. Then, and only then, did I get off the chair, grab my cell phone, and make the phone call I'd been dreaming of making since I'd first entered that kitchen.

"Alex, it's Hope. I'm in the basement kitchen at the Thorndales. I've got a woman tied up who just confessed to killing Pimsey, and I've got myself one very expensive painting. And please hurry because my head hurts really, really bad."

CHAPTER 32

Alex insisted I have Dr. Bridges look at my arm and my head, and Dr. Bridges insisted I spend a night in the hospital for observation. But *I* insisted to both of them that spending a night in the hospital was nonsense because I had a big story to finish.

I worked on my story the rest of that day, and by that night, I had emailed it to Earl Denton.

My phone rang not long after. "Is every single thing in this story true?" Earl asked me.

"Every single thing," I said.

"Hope . . . that's one helluva story."

"A good-enough-for-a-raise kind of story?"

"Oh, heck, no. But good enough to get your expenses covered from here on out."

It was a start. And more importantly, maybe the story was good enough to attract the attention of one of the big-city newspapers.

When the next morning rolled around, I really wanted to stay in bed for the rest of my life. But I had a job to do.

It was Thursday, and I had a deadline to meet. A deadline that had been looming for almost thirteen years.

I woke up early, hauled my aching arm and half-broken cranium over to Granny's house, and started painting.

At noon, Katie and her children showed up. But not to hassle me. They were there with sodas and burgers and extra brushes and another ladder. They were there to work.

And that evening, Juan and April and Carlos stopped by to give me a hand as well.

"Is everything cool with Uncle Juan?" I asked April.

"Much cooler than I thought," she said. "He wasn't happy at first, but he was also glad to know that Carlos is doing okay and that I'm happy to see him. And Uncle Juan said that after this week, he realizes that nothing is more important than family. And that means *all* of our family."

"Good. And April, I talked to Sheriff Kramer, and I told him about your involvement. He says you didn't do anything wrong. But he asks that next time someone asks you to paint a replica of a famous painting, just run it by him first."

She laughed. "I will. Thank you, Hope."

The next day, Friday, Katie's husband, Chris, took the day off from work and joined our growing paint crew. And on Saturday morning, the sheriff of Hopeless himself, Alex Kramer, showed up with even more reinforcements. Molly Scratchett, and to my complete surprise, none other than Mortimer Snoot.

"Snoot?" I said as he walked over with a goofy smile on his face.

He shrugged. "Sheriff says if it wasn't for you, I'd be living with a bunch of murderers in the state prison by now. I thought helping was the least I could do."

I gave him a big hug.

"I want to say officially that I was a big pain when I was in high school, that you were right to be mad, and that I will never, ever kick you in the Ben and Jerrys ever again."

I turned to Mrs. Scratchett. "And how about you? How'd the sheriff convince you to come out and join us?"

She waved a hand dismissively. "He didn't need to convince me. When he told me how you rammed old Hannah in her belly, I thought to myself, that is my kind of chick. I thought we could hang out, smoke some menthols, and drink Busch Light sometime."

"Mrs. Scratchett, you are one classy lady."

I think that made her day.

We finished painting the house at eleven forty-five a.m. on Saturday. Just shy of thirteen years since Granny and I made our little wager.

When Granny came home from the bar, she examined the job. Very slowly. Very carefully. As if looking for a reason to claim I hadn't done what I'd promised. Finally, she turned to me.

"Well, granddaughter, it looks like you proved me wrong. You got the house painted after all. Although I'm not sure I expected a small army to be helping you . . . but a deal's a deal."

She took her wallet out of her back pocket, counted out one hundred and seventy-five dollars, and held it out to me.

"I don't want your money," I said, pushing her hand away. "I didn't do this for the money."

She laughed. "And I never for a moment thought you'd actually accept it. But I'm proud of you, Hope. You saw this through. And there's something else. I may have mentioned that I wasn't sure how tough you were. Katie told me how everything went down in the Thorndales' kitchen, and I have to say, you might be the toughest girl I have ever met."

"Thanks, Granny."

As she walked off, Alex Kramer came over to me with two cold beers. "You ready for one?" he asked me. "We never did get to share that drink at the Thorndales' party."

I grabbed the beer from him and clinked his bottle with mine. "I'm ready for *more* than one. Although I have to warn you, the guests at *my* big party are pretty refined."

He looked around. Dominic was flicking paint off the end of his brush at his sister. Mrs. Scratchett, cigarette dangling from her lips, was showing Chris how she could crush a beer can against her forehead. Katie was peering down the back of Celia's diaper. Granny was snapping a towel at Mr. Snoot's butt while Bess looked on in amusement.

"Yep, you run a very sophisticated affair, Hope Walker. Listen . . . about some of the stuff I said back at the Thorndale house . . ."

"You were right."

"I'm not so sure about that. A bet's a bet. You won. And what's more, you're one hell of an investigator."

"Well, as long as I'm allowed to blindly accuse people of crimes against humanity."

He laughed. "Yes, as long as you're allowed that."

"I'm sorry for being such a pain in the butt."

"And I'm sorry for acting like a jerk."

For a moment, his brilliant green eyes met mine, and I thought my heart would stop. Then I forced my mouth to say something.

"Does that mean I get to investigate crimes?"

He nodded. "Yes. As long as we stay out of each other's way."

I wasn't sure I wanted to stay out of Alex Kramer's way. But all I said was, "I think I can handle that."

Katie came toward us with Celia in one arm and a paper bag in the other. She winked at me, and I smiled at Alex.

"Alex, I hope you don't mind," I said, "but Katie and I did some research. It seems that sheriffs have quite a bit of leeway when it comes to their uniform."

"My uniform?"

"Yes," Katie said. "Apparently, you don't have to wear the same clothes as Ed Kline and look like a total dipstick."

"What Katie's trying to say is, we looked around for something that you might find a little more comfortable."

Katie handed him the bag. "And we'd like you to go try it on."

"What—now?"

"Yes, now," I said. "And if you don't, Katie will let Dominic spend Monday in your jail cell. All day Monday."

"Say no more." Alex took the bag and went into Granny's house.

That's when I saw Wilma Jenkins getting out of her silver Lexus.

"Hey, Mayor Jenkins," Granny yelled. "You heard that my house got a fresh coat of paint and now you want to buy me out for a million dollars, am I right?"

Wilma smiled sweetly. "Oh, Granny, I could never afford to buy your house. Actually, I'd like to speak to Hope."

Granny turned to me. "I assume you can handle yourself?"

I nodded and walked over to Wilma.

"So, what are you doing here?" I asked.

"The word down at Buck's is that you painted Granny's house for a hundred and seventy-five dollars because you're dead broke. And I thought, how terrible. Especially considering you're going to try to buy an expensive piece of real estate in the near future. So I want to help you out."

"I'm sure you do."

"Yes, I figured that with inflation, painting Granny's house is worth at least twice what it was thirteen years ago." She pulled a wad of cash from her bag and held it out to me. "So here's another one seventy-five to help you out, since you need it so badly."

She smiled as if she had me right where she wanted me.

"Wilma, with no due respect at all, I think you know what you can do with your money."

"I sort of thought you were going to react that way, which makes what I'm about to say even more fun. The real estate world is very small, you know. And I thought it was my duty to call your apartment building in Portland and explain your personal situation. Naturally, the owners agreed that giving you your deposit back would be an awfully big mistake."

"*You're* the reason I lost my deposit?"

She smiled. "You see, Hope. I told you not to go to war with me. I promise, you will lose every single time." She winked as she turned back toward her car. "Have a great weekend!"

I resisted the urge to throw a rock at the back of her head. Instead, I spun around to get myself another beer.

But what I saw when I turned toward Granny's house was Sheriff Alex Kramer walking out in his new uniform. Blue jeans, cowboy boots, a cowboy hat, and a long brown leather coat with a single gold star on it.

"Holy smokes," I said.

Thankfully, Katie was there with that second beer. "Doesn't look so dorky now, does he?"

"Looks like Hot Alex is back."

Katie clinked her beer bottle with mine. "And if you ever tell my husband I bought Alex an outfit just so he'd look hot around the office, I will tell everyone about that thing on your toe."

"You wouldn't."

"I think you know me better than that. You up for hiking next week?"

"Are you serious?"

"No, but how else am I going to get in shape?"

"I'll bring a bucket of fried chicken."

"And that's why you're my best friend."

I walked over to Alex. "Looking good, Sheriff."

"I do, don't I?" He grinned. "I feel much better in these clothes. Thank you."

"You're welcome."

"What was Mayor Jenkins talking to you about?" He looked past me toward the street.

"Oh, that was nothing."

"It didn't look like nothing."

I shrugged. "Turns out Wilma's trying to pick a fight with a girl."

"And?"

I smiled. "She picked the wrong girl."

DEAR READER: A NOTE FROM DANIEL CARSON

Thank you for reading *A Hopeless Heist*, the second book in the Hope Walker Mysteries. The third Hope Walker Mystery, *A Hopeless Discovery*, will be released in late January of 2019. If you sign up for my newsletter, I will send you an update when the third book is available.

Daniel Carson Newsletter Link: **http://eepurl.com/dtZWfH**

FIRST, I wanted to apologize to those readers who were expecting Book 2 in late July of 2018. I'm sorry. It just didn't happen. A combination of summer, and children, and goats, and ball bearings. Don't ask about the goats. But the good news is, the fetzer valve got fixed, I've got a new book production schedule, and I should be able to make this one. Promise! That means Book 3 in late January and Book 4 in late March. I thank you so much for your patience.

Second, I appreciate everybody who has reached out to me directly or left a review on Amazon.com or on Goodreads about how much they enjoyed Book 1. I really do appreciate it. My promise is to try to write the best book I can each time out. For me and the folks of Hopeless, Idaho, that means mystery, humor, a quirky town, and lovable characters.

At least, that's my hope!

Reminder to sign up for my newsletter if you want updates, or you can always come over to my Facebook Author page and say hello. I would love to hear from you.

Daniel Carson Facebook Page: **https://www.facebook.com/AuthorDanielCarson/**

AND REMEMBER that Hope Walker Three: *A Hopeless Discovery* comes out in late January.

Thank you so much for reading!

Daniel

P.S. REVIEWS ARE AWESOME. If you could leave a short review on Amazon, I would be thrilled. If you could leave a review on the front page of the *New York Times,* I would be overjoyed.

Update: Books in the Hope Walker Series as of August 2020

Season 1

Book 1: *A Hopeless Murder*

Book 2: *A Hopeless Heist*

Book 3: *A Hopeless Discovery*

Book 4: *A Hopeless Game*

Book 5: *A Hopeless Christmas*
Season 2

Book 6: *A Hopeless Journey*

. . .

Book 7: *A Hopeless Valentine (Coming Fall 2020)*

Book 8: *A Hopeless Sheriff (Release TBD)*

Book 9: *A Hopeless Barbecue (Release TBD)*

Book 10: *A Hopeless Storm (Release TBD)*

Made in United States
Troutdale, OR
04/03/2024